Sent From Heaven 2

Dee Dee M. Scott

I0623852

Ahsyad Publication

www.ahsyadpublication.com

Sent From Heaven 2

ISBN-13: 978-0615929026

ISBN-10: 0615929028

Dedication:

To my mom and dad, the late Joseph & Kathy Paul Gregg. For Aunt Dean, who always shared her favorite Cream of Mushroom soup with me. You made me feel very special when I was a little girl and for that I'll always love you! RIP!

Acknowledgments: First and foremost to my foundation: Jehovah God & Jesus Christ. Without you, my life is useless. I thank you for life, health, peace of mind, and the gift of writing. To my best friend and Husband, Danny Scott for always supporting me no matter what, and for keeping the promise you made to my mother before her death.

To my children: I love you with all my heart!!!

To the readers and supporters: thank you!

God bless!

Prologue

Miami Florida

Karalee took in her empty apartment. Everything of value was gone. Her home had been burglarized. She searched for evidence that the thief might still be in the residence, but everything was eerily quiet and there were no signs of forced entry. The alarm hadn't gone off either.

It had to be an inside job, Karalee thought. Someone who knew her had done this. But she had no friends. On the other hand, her Fiancé, Chris, always had different people coming in and out of their apartment being he was an aspiring actor. Had he unknowingly let someone get the code to their security system? They'd always been so careful, and the neighborhood they lived in was safe too. There had been a few car break-ins over the past year, but nothing to panic over.

Trembling, Karalee opened her purse and searched for her Blackberry. She knew she should call the police, but instead she called Chris. He was at a meeting with his talent agent, Brenda Myers. Brenda had signed Chris to her agency three months ago, and he was already getting small acting roles on television. Today, he'd been called in to do a second reading for an upcoming movie. There was a good possibility that he would get the role. If he did, his career would really take off. She would be right next to her man as he walked the red carpet.

Karalee hated to call and interrupt him with this bad news. He was going to be just as pissed as her that someone had broken into their apartment. She picked up the hammer from the floor just in case the crook was still inside. Snatching out her cell, she hit Chris's number that was programmed on her phone. It went straight to voicemail.

"Hello, this is Chris. Leave a message and I'll get back to you."

She blushed. His deep, sexy voice always made her hot. However, now was not the time or the place to be distracted by her man. This was serious.

"Chris, baby," Karalee said, breathing hard into the phone. "When you get this message, call me. It's an emergency."

She ended the message and dialed 911. She heard a recording telling her to remain on the line. She cursed. Someone could have been trying to kill her for Pete's sake. She moved deeper into the ransacked apartment. The living room and dining room set were gone. So were the expensive art pieces from the walls. Even the computers and big screen television had been stolen.

She raced to her bedroom. The only thing left was a table that had belonged to her late grandmother. Her heart ached as she headed for the closet. She searched through her clothes. She found her wedding dress, hidden at the back. "Thank God," she whispered, placing a hand over her thudding heart.

It had taken six months for her to find the perfect dress. She and Chris were getting married in two weeks. They were also moving into their new dream home. She knew she would not feel safe in the apartment anymore. There was someone other than herself to think about. Smiling, she placed a hand over her stomach. A small bulge was beginning to form. She and Chris were having a baby! Yesterday, the doctor had told her that she was six weeks pregnant. She would share the good news with Chris on their honeymoon.

Karalee looked over the empty bedroom. Her heart ached. They would have to buy new furniture. She and Chris had discussed buying new furniture in the past, but had decided against it because she didn't have a steady job. The only jobs she'd had were under the table ones. She hadn't worked a nine to five since the unthinkable had happened at eighteen and she'd served six months in prison. Now, Chris was supporting her and paying for everything, including her mother's rehab bills.

Moving to Chris's closet, she noticed it was completely empty. Wooden hangers stared back at her.

She closed her eyes and sighed. It had taken Chris years to collect his expensive shoes and suits. Even his jewelry box was gone.

There was a loud crash. She almost jumped out of her skin. Quickly, she jerked around with the hammer tightly in her hand. Scanning the room, she noticed it was her overweight cat. She had knocked over a picture of her and Chris that had been on the table. She rushed to the cat and took her into her arms, rubbing her silky fur. "Snow White, I'm happy they didn't steal you." The cat purred and licked her paw.

She picked up the picture from the floor. Chris had taken it the day she and him had graduated from college. He'd whisked her away on a romantic vacation to the Bahamas afterwards.

She smiled. She was so blessed to have a man like him. He was going to be a great father to their baby. With Snow White in her arms, she moved back to the kitchen. 911 hadn't answered yet. She turned on the phone's speaker and placed it on the granite countertop.

A blinking light, under a pile of papers on the living room floor caught her attention. She put Snow White down and moved to the light. It was the answering machine. She pressed the play button and headed back to the kitchen. Chris's voice stopped her dead in her tracks.

"Karalee; I really don't know where or how to begin. I moved out and I'm not coming back. I've been trying to get the courage to do this for years. I wanted to tell you in person, but I knew you would try to stop me, so I waited until you went to visit your mother in rehab to move my things out. I'm relocating to New York to pursue my acting career. It's now or never. I'm 34 and I'm not getting any younger. I want to make something out of my life and be more than a computer programmer. My talent agent, Brenda, thinks I have a shot at making it. I need to see if I can. Please don't be angry. I can't go through with the wedding and live a lie. I just don't want to wake up twenty years from now and wonder what if. I've taken care of you and your mother for long enough. It's time for me to do something for myself. I do love you, but being tied down to a 9 to 5 is killing me. You can keep the apartment. The rent is paid up until the first and so are the other bills. I also left you some money in the pantry. I hope you can move on and find it in your heart to forgive me. You are a good woman and I'm sure some man will be lucky to have you. Unfortunately, that man is not me."

Karalee leaned on the counter for support. Hot tears raced down her cheeks, and her hands were trembling. Her stomach began to cramp. At first, the cramps were light, but then they became unbearable. Sobbing, she collapsed to the floor and curled up in pain.

She noticed bright red blood on her hands. It was coming from underneath her skirt. "My baby!" she cried, holding her stomach as the blood flow increased. The voice of the 911 operator brought her from her shock. Weakly, she stood and picked up the cell.

"911, what's the nature of your emergency?"

"I need an ambulance," Karalee moaned before collapsing to the floor.

1

Atlanta Georgia

TWO MONTHS LATER

Karalee pulled into the shrub lined driveway of her sister's one-level brick home. "Thank God I made it," she mumbled, before shutting off the engine of her 1985 GMC short bed truck. Unlike Chris, the truck she'd had since high school had never let her down. She was glad she had not gotten rid of it when Chris had brought her the brand new Range Rover last Christmas.

She pulled out her cell phone and wrote a text message to Chris. She told him she was no longer in Florida and had moved back home to Atlanta. She stared at the text and debated on whether or not to send it. Over the past two months she had sent him several texts, including one when she'd been admitted to the hospital after suffering a miscarriage. He had not responded. She was sure he would not reply back to this text either. She pressed the end button and dropped her head.

Without him she felt like her life had been stripped of meaning. She couldn't stop dwelling on what had went wrong, and what could have been. The pain she constantly felt was excruciating. She didn't think she would ever be happy again. Still, she was determined to hold her head high and handle her business. No tears would fall from her eyes. She was strong, and she refused to stay down and feel sorry for herself.

Snow White distracted her by hopping onto her lap. The truck had no air conditioner and the June heat was unbearable. "So how do you like Hotlanta?" she asked Snow white. The cat purred like she understood her question. Karalee laughed before reality settled back in.

Never in a million years had she thought she'd return back to ATL, or be single at the age of thirty-three. But after Chris left, the eviction notice arrived. Her jeep was repossessed, and the bills started piling up. The under the table jobs dried up. She tried applying for nine to five work being it was her responsibility to pay for her mother's rehab bills. But after she revealed that she'd served six months in prison, the employers never called back. It didn't matter that she was multilingual and had a degree in marketing and finance; a criminal record just didn't mix with corporate America.

She would have gladly continued applying for work, and searching for under the table jobs to support her mother. But two weeks after Chris left, her mother ditched rehab and disappeared. She knew it was time for her to leave Miami then.

Her sister, Summer, had invited her to stay with her. She'd accepted the offer even though she hated Atlanta.

There were too many sour memories from a past that she wanted to forget.

Quickly, she checked her face in the rear view mirror. She didn't want her sister to see her looking like a hot mess even though she was going through pure hell.

Sure enough, she looked just like she felt. Her almond shaped eyes were fire red, and her cinnamon toned skin had lost its glow. Bags were underneath her eyes, and her naturally curly hair was a mess being she'd had to keep the windows down the entire ride.

Just as she was about to exit the truck, she noticed her sister's front door swing open. She smiled as Summer swiftly walked to the truck.

Summer hadn't changed one bit. She was a year younger, but both looked exactly like their mother with their mile long legs and dangerous curves. The only difference between them was their hair and makeup. Karalee was all natural, while Summer wore tons of makeup and laced front wigs. Due to Lupus, Summer's hair had thinned out and caused her skin to develop butterfly rashes.

Summer smiled and batted her fake eyelashes. "Girl, why didn't you blow the horn and let me know you were out here?"

"I would have if the horn worked." Karalee unbuckled the seatbelt while Summer tried to open the driver's door.

"Don't bother. It's jammed-shut." Karalee climbed out of the truck through the passenger door.

"You need to junk this old thing," Summer said, before pulling her into a tight hug that threatened to cut off her circulation.

Karalee pulled away and kissed her on the cheek. "Hey, grandma gave me this truck before she died. This old thing has been with me through thick and thin. I'm never giving it up."

"But you are gonna park that eye sore in the garage, right?"

Karalee smiled. "Just as soon as I get my bags and grandma's table."

"You still have that too?"

"Oh yeah. Unlike people, the old things grandma gave me weathered the storm."

"And what about this cat?"

"Can she stay indoors, please?"

"I guess. She is pretty." Summer proceeded to pick the cat up.

Snow White hissed and backed up.

Summer frowned. "What's up with your cat?"

"She has to get use to you," Karalee said, taking the fat cat into her arms to calm her. "She has a bad temper and a dirty habit of scratching people she doesn't know well."

Summer frowned and grabbed a suitcase from the back of the truck. "Well, please keep your 'cat from hell' away from me."

Karalee grabbed the other suitcase and followed her.

"Hurry up," Summer ordered. "There's somebody I'd like for you to meet."

"Oh Lord," Karalee exhaled. "Please don't let it be another one of your boyfriends. You change men like you change your panties."

Summer smirked. "I see you still speak your mind."

"I wouldn't be me if I didn't," Karalee answer back. She took in the gorgeous one level home located in the beautiful cul-de-sac. It was two minutes away from downtown Atlanta. Considering their turbulent childhood, Summer had done very well for herself. Her yard was manicured and well kept. Inside the spacious house was just as breathtaking. There was an entrance hall, a spacious living room with built in bookcases, a gas log fireplace, and stainless steel appliances in the kitchen. The furniture throughout was both stylish and comfortable.

Karalee closed her eyes and inhaled the delicious aroma of basil and Italian seasoning wafting through the air. Her stomach growled.

"I cooked your favorite."

"Spaghetti?"

"Yep, and buttered garlic bread with salad on the side." Summer glanced over at Karalee. "You look like you could use a good meal. You lost weight?"

"Stress and a Ramen noodle diet will do it to you every time."

Summer looked at her sympathetically. "Well, you're gonna put that weight back on as much as I cook."

They walked down a flight of stairs and Summer opened the basement door. She let Karalee enter first. "I want you to have complete privacy, so I'm letting you take the basement room. I hope you like it."

Karalee smiled sadly. "This is nice." It looked like a miniature apartment being there was a sitting area with a loveseat and television. She had her own bathroom and a door where she could go into the backyard. There was even a mini kitchen with a small refrigerator and microwave, and the queen-sized bed looked comfortable. Still, Karalee was remembering her life with Chris. She hated him for hurting her.

Summer hugged her. "Sis, I hate you going through this. You still love him, don't you?"

Karalee shook her head. Her emotions wanted to spilled over, but she'd never let anyone see her sweat, or worse yet, cry. "I'm fine," she mumbled.

Summer gawked at her. "Fine? Girl, you had a miscarriage because of him." Summer shook her head. "It's okay to hurt, Karalee. There is nothing wrong with crying and feeling sad about what happened. Stop holding your pain in. That's not good. One day you are going to break down."

Karalee placed on a forced smile and moved away. "I'm fine. Time heals all wounds."

Summer looked at her for few seconds in uncertainty before she spoke. "Well, there's a man out there way better waiting for you. Chris will find just what he's looking for in those streets. When he realizes what he let go, he'll regret it."

"Please, can we talk about something other than Chris?" Karalee asked, placing her suitcase on the bed.

Summer looked dejected, but she quickly changed the subject. "My friend's birthday is today. She's having a big party later on tonight? Why don't you come with me? Who knows, you might find a good man there who can help you out."

Karalee rolled her eyes heavenward. "I don't want a man helping me. That's exactly why I'm in this situation now."

Summer frowned. "No, you're in this situation because Chris took all of your things. You should find him and take his butt to court."

"For what?" Karalee asked. "Everything in that apartment belonged to him". She shook her head. "This taught me a big lesson. I'm never depending on a man for anything. I'm going to be completely independent and stand on my own feet. I'm going to find a job and get my own place for me and mama too."

"Mama?" Summer repeated in a strain voice.

"Yes. I'm worried sick about her. She's still somewhere in Florida. She ditched rehab and I don't know where she's at. None of her friends have seen her either."

Summer placed a hand on her shoulder. "Mama's doing what she does best: getting high and stealing. If you ask me, you need to forget about her. That woman has hurt you enough."

Karalee dragged in a deep breath. She didn't understand why Summer couldn't see that their mother was ill. Her mother's life had been hard and she needed help, not hate.

Summer placed the other suitcase on the bed and sat. "Listen; let's not even focus on mama, okay? Right now we're gonna concentrate on getting you back on your feet. You need a job."

"I sure do," Karalee agreed. "But no one will hire me with my criminal record."

Summer clasped her hands together on her lap and smiled. "I have connections."

"What sort of connections?"

Summer sniffed the air. "Wait right here." She moved from the bed and headed for the door. "Let me check the oven. Something is burning."

Karalee began to unpack while she waited. A few minutes later, she felt a presence behind her. She knew Summer was back in the room. "So, what were you saying about a job?" she asked, folding a pair of jeans.

Unexpectedly, a hand slapped her hard on the butt.

She jerked around, dropping the pants to the floor.

A man stood behind her with caramel skin and shoulder length dreads in his head. He was smiling and licking his lips.

"What in the hell is your problem?" Karalee shouted, her chest heaving.

"My bad," the man said. He held his hands up in surrender and slowly took a step backwards. "I thought you were Summer."

Karalee pointed her finger at him. "You know damn well I wasn't Summer!" She was about to say something to wipe the silly grin off his face when Summer entered the room.

The man gave Summer a sloppy kiss. She giggled like a schoolgirl when he pulled away.

"Baby, you didn't tell me your sister was here," the man said, licking his lips again. "She sure is fine," he added. His eyes roamed over Karalee's body.

Summer punched him playfully on the shoulder. "Watch it," she warned before focusing back on Karalee. "I want you to meet my fiancé, Spider."

"Your fiancé?" Karalee asked, her eyes widening.

"Yes." Summer showed her the small ring on her index finger.

"Well, you're fiancé just smacked me on the butt," Karalee growled.

"I thought she was you, baby," Spider said, stuttering as he tried to explain. "She looks just like you from behind. You both got those curves." He stroked his chin, while he stared lustfully at Karalee's hips.

Summer blushed, but Karalee wanted to gag.

"Please accept my apology, sister- in- law," Spider said with the same stupid grin on his face.

Karalee's left brow elevated. "You're not married to my sister yet, so don't call me that."

Spider smiled. "No problem, pretty lady."

Summer cleared her throat. "Spider, I just realized we are out of parmesan cheese, and I don't have a dessert. Can you go to the store and get it for me?"

"With what money?"Spider asked, taking a sip of his drink.

Summer looked embarrassed. "Get a twenty from my purse."

Spider smiled. "Where your car keys?"

"On the kitchen table."

"I'ma use your cell phone too, baby." Spider hugged her waist. "Mines out of minutes."

"Okay," Summer said, pushing him toward the door.

Before Spider left, he pulled Summer close. He squeezed her butt and gave her another sloppy kiss. Only this time his lustful eyes were directly on Karalee.

Disgusted, Karalee looked away. Already she did not like him.

"Nice meeting you soon to be sister- in- law," Spider said, before exiting the room.

Karalee rolled her eyes and went back to unpacking. "Where did you find this one?" she asked.

"Pauline's Waffles and Chicken." Summer looked dreamy eyed. "He was working drive thru and we hit it off."

"Well; at least this one has a job." Karalee didn't knock anyone who was trying. She knew exactly how hard it was being she'd been jobless for so long.

"He did have a job," Summer wearily admitted. "That fool overslept this morning and was fired."

Karalee sucked her teeth.

"Anyway, he makes me happy and we're getting married. You know; I've been praying for a good man for years and I finally met him. We connected like that." Summer snapped her fingers. "He's trying to get his GED. He wants to open his own barbershop too. My baby can cut some hair, and he treats me good which is more than I can say about the other fools before him. He's the one. I know it."

Karalee shook her head. Her sister was just as excited about this man as she had been about the other men before him. She didn't understand her sister anymore than she understood Chinese. She was a college graduate with a beautiful home and nice car. She'd even had a good job before she'd gotten sick with Lupus. Still, she continued to pick losers who she ended up taking care of.

"Anyway, I'll tell you all about Spider later." Summer interrupted her thoughts. "Let's talk about this job."

Karalee forgot all about Spider as she sat on the bed. "What kind of job?"

"As a personal assistant at the place I used to work."

"That sounds great, but what about my criminal record? They'll never look past that."

"Sure they will," Summer said, smiling. "My friend Renee, who's having that birthday party tonight, is the manager in human resources. I'll talk to her later. I'm sure she'll overlook your record. "

"Where is it that you used to work again?" Karalee asked, excited for the first time in months.

Summer smiled. "Tucker Insurance."

***

Marcus Tucker moved inside the boxing ring with ease and confidence. The sweat cascading down his sculptured body made the tattoo on the left side of his abdomen glisten. Outside of the ring, a group of scantily clad women were eyeballing him. A smile creased his striking face. They wanted him. With the snap of a finger, he could have his pick. But he wasn't interested.

In the past, he'd had his share of those types of women. Every night there'd been a new date. Until that lifestyle had caught up with him, and he'd almost lost everything.

Now, he was older and wiser. He'd learned that most of the women he encountered didn't love Marcus Tucker the man; they loved Marcus Tucker who had ownership in a multi-billion-dollar Insurance corporation.

To get next to him, women pretended to be whatever they thought he wanted them to be. Later, their true intentions would come out and he would feel used.

Due to that, he'd never been able to give his heart fully to a woman. He didn't believe he'd ever find a woman who would give him true love and happiness either. He was content being single.

Marcus focused his concentration back on the action inside of the ring. "Punch me," he encouraged Tony, the young man sparing with him.

Tony took a deep breath before landing a hard blow to his eight pack stomach.

Marcus felt his belly tighten. His brown eyes twinkled and he smiled, displaying a set of pearly white teeth. "Harder," he ordered. He pointed to his chiseled chest. "I want you to release your frustrations and anger right here."

Tony landed three more blows to his toned abdomen, and the two continued bouncing inside the ring.

Second Chance Gym & Fitness was filled with young men between the ages of thirteen through twenty this Sunday afternoon. Years ago, Marcus had opened the exercise room for disadvantaged teens as a place for them to release stress and to help them stay out of trouble.

At one time, he'd been a troubled young man who couldn't control his anger. Fortunately, his ninth grade teacher had introduced him to boxing. He'd never gone pro and had no desire to do so, but because of the sport, he was able to release his aggravation and fury. It had saved his life. So it was a no-brainer for him to open a gym and do the same for other troubled teens in the community, including seventeen year old Tony.

Tony came from a poor, single parent home and was constantly getting into fights at school. His mother had signed him up at the gym as a last resort to save him. Marcus had been working with Tony for six months and had seen some improvements with his behavior, but last week he'd gotten into another fight that had caused him to get suspended from school. Marcus would make him pay for that now.

"Punch me again," Marcus ordered.

"I'm too tired," Tony complained.

"That's great," Marcus said sarcastically, before punching him in the chest. "Maybe now you won't have the energy to get into any more fights at school."

"I won't," Tony promised, trying to keep his tired arms up.

Marcus smiled and punched him again. "Do I have your word?"

"Yes sir. No more fights."

"Unless it's with me or the punching bag," Marcus said. "I want you to graduate this year, got it?"

Tony nodded and continued boxing with Marcus for the next several minutes.

Just as Marcus was about to call it quits, the tinted double doors to the gym opened. His sister Emily strolled inside dressed in her Sunday best. He couldn't help but to notice how out of place she looked at the gym. She was naturally classy and her features were soft. However, there was nothing spongy about Emily Tucker. She was one tough cookie.

After the untimely death of their mother, Emily became the leader over him and his four brothers. She taught them to stick together and that there was nothing more important than family.   She also educated them about the family business.

Emily was the President and CEO of Tucker insurance, one of the largest African American Insurance agencies in the U.S. The company had been started by their father in a small, one room building with less than 3 people on the payroll. After his dad retired, Emily, he and his brothers took over. However, Emily became the helm of the business. Due to her intelligence, the company had

expanded to fifteen states, had ten International offices, and nearly nine hundred employees.

Marcus took off his boxing gloves. He knew something important had transpired for Emily to visit him at his gym on a Sunday. Sabbath was family church day, and she and his four brothers faithfully went to the place of worship. But not him. He hadn't stepped foot inside a church since the day of his mother's funeral.

"Alright, you're done for the day," he told Tony. "I will check in with your mother next week to see how you're doing at school. I expect a good report."

Tony nodded before he moved to mingle with the other young men, scattered around the gym.

Marcus stepped outside of the ring, but before he could proceed to Emily, he dropped his towel. The group of women who'd been watching him box earlier stopped in front of him. The one with exotic green eyes picked the towel up and placed it across his shoulder. She gave him a folded piece of paper. He opened it and noticed her number, written in red lipstick.

"Call me," she purred in a heavy Island accent, before she and the other ladies moved away.

Marcus stroked his trimmed goatee as he observed her switching away. He wouldn't call her. She was pretty, but good looks were no longer enough to pull him in. He wanted a woman who could stimulate him intellectually and emotionally. Plus, he knew her type. She was trouble with a capital "T". Still, he was a man. He loved looking and enjoyed the attention even more.

"Ahem!" Emily interrupted. She folded her arms across her chest and glared at the women who were now near the snack machine. "I see you have fans," she said sourly.

"I'm used to it," Marcus said nonchalantly. He crumbled the paper the green eyed beauty had given him and tossed it into the trash bin.

"Are you bragging?" Emily asked.

"Not at all," Marcus answered while towering his torso dry. "It's common. Nothing to get excited about. Women throw themselves at me all the time."

"And you take advantage of it; don't you, playa?"

"Hey; you taught me to respect women, remember?" Marcus winked his eye at her. "And for the record: I don't play women."

"You used to," Emily said sneakily.

"No, never," he corrected. "I always let women know what they were getting into and told them upfront that I wasn't looking for anything serious. That's the difference."

"And that makes you what? A saint?"

"No, but that does make me honest," Marcus shot back. He flexed his muscles and the women stared at him like a pack of starving wolves ready to attack.

Emily rolled her eyes and sat on a chair near the ring.

"So what brings you here on a Sunday?" Marcus asked, giving her a peck on the cheek.

"We have business to discuss."

"Is it so important that you couldn't wait until you see me at the office tomorrow?" He sat next to her and broke the seal on his bottled water. Five days a week

Marcus headed the Marketing and advertising department at Tucker Insurance. He did everything from managing worldwide sales to casting models for commercials. However, on the weekends, the business was the last thing on his mind. He didn't want to hear anything about it. He loved to relax at his gym.

"Yes, it is very important." Emily appeared serious. "I want to make sure that you have everything in order at home being you're about to become a father."

Marcus choked on his water. His large eyes grew wide and flashed with fear. He thought that maybe he'd heard Emily wrong. After all, he'd just had a tough workout. "Where did you hear that?" he asked, glaring at the society paper tucked underneath her arm that she read faithfully. Emily was about to say something, but he didn't give her a chance to speak. "I'm sure it came straight out of that silly paper. I hope you know the majority of the stories they print in that crap about the Tucker men are false."

"Oh really?" Emily leaned forward and stared him straight in the eyes. "Did the society paper lie when they printed that article about you getting into motorcycle accidents three times in the last six months?"

"Okay, so they told the truth three times."

"More like four or five times," Emily muttered.

"Well, that story about me expecting a child is B.S, "Marcus barked. "I haven't slept with a woman in almost a year." He lowered his gaze as his ex flashed before his eyes.

"Well, thank you for divulging that bit of disgusting information." Emily shook her head. "But I think you and I got our wires mixed up somewhere during this conversation."

"So what in the heck do you mean I'm about to become a father?" he asked, wiping the newly accumulated sweat from his face.

"You're going to be a father figure, silly," Emily clarified. She hit him playfully on the back of the head.

Still confused, he massaged the spot on his low cut hair that Emily had smacked.

"Don't tell me you forgot about Carlos?"

Marcus closed his eyes briefly. He'd had so much going on with work and his personal life that his first cousin had slipped his mind. His eyes flashed with uncertainty. "I don't think it's a good idea for Carlos to come live with me."

"What do you mean?" Emily looked displeased. "Carlos was mamas only sister's son. He is family, and Tucker's-"

"Take care of family." Marcus finished the sentence for her. "Believe me; I know that better than you and our brothers. I took care of all of you when mom died."

Emily lowered her eyes. "Yes, you did. You were our protector, and you did a damn good job too." She looked at him again. "That's why I know you will take good care of Carlos. He's been through so much since aunt Emma passed away. It would really lift his spirits if he could be with you during this difficult time. Remember how you felt when mom died?"

Marcus eyes darkened as parts of his teenage years flashed before him. He didn't want to think about how hurt he'd been when he'd learned his mother had suffered a heart attack and died. He'd been fourteen at the time and his entire world had fallen apart. He'd had to grow up quickly and being that he was the oldest boy, a lot of responsibility had been placed on him. Due to that, he hadn't had much of a childhood. Now, he didn't want to be tied down. He didn't even want to have children of his own.

"I just don't want him to go through what we did," Emily said, bringing him from his troubled thoughts. When mom closed her eyes-"

"We went through hell," Marcus cut her off sharply. He turned away from Emily, not wanting to go down memory lane now or ever again. It only made him furious, and he'd come too far with his temper and anger issues to revert back to the old him. "Why can't he stay with you and Stanley," Marcus asked, referring to Emily's husband of the past sixteen years.

"I offered, but he wants to stay with you. You know how much he admires you. Every since he was a little boy he's tried to be just like you."

"I know." Marcus smiled sadly and faced her again. "He's a great young man."

"So what's the issue?"

"I just don't think I can handle a teenager."

"You handle these knuckle heads in this gym. What would be so different?"

"The fact that I can send them home to their parents at the end of the day," Marcus retorted sarcastically. "If I let Carlos stay with me he will be my responsibility 24/7 and I'm not sure I can handle that."

Emily stood slowly from her seat.

"Hey; where are you going?"

"I'm leaving," Emily announced.

"But we were in the middle of a conversation."

"There's nothing further to discuss. You don't want to take care of Carlos. I guess I'll tell him the news. It's really going to break his heart when he learns he has to stay with me, but so be it."

Emily gave him a kiss on the cheek and proceeded to walk away.

Marcus shook his head. Guilt settled on his chest like heavy bricks as he watched her leave. He called out for her just as she was about to open the door. She turned and began moving back toward him.

"When is Carlos scheduled to arrive?"

"In two weeks. Why?"

"I'll pick him up from the airport."

Emily's eyes lit up. "So that means you'll let Carlos stay with you?"

Marcus nodded.

Emily gave him a tight hug. "Thank you! Carlos is going to be elated."

Marcus pulled away from her tight embraced. "Hold on a minute." He folded his arms across his chest. "I'm going to need your help."

"Done. I will certainly help out. He can stay with me every weekend. Plus your new personal assistant will be starting tomorrow. I'm sure that will help you out a lot."

"I don't want a personal assistant meddling in my private affairs," Marcus huffed.

"Just try her out," Emily said, rolling her eyes upward.

"You're going to need help with things around your house, and this gym being you'll have to devout a lot of time to Carlos. She can work from your office until you get to know her and feel comfortable. She starts tomorrow."

"Tomorrow?"

"Yes; the timing is perfect. She can help you out with the auditions."

Marcus looked confused again.

"Don't tell me you forgot about the auditions too?

Marcus hit his head playfully. "I have so much going on; it completely slipped my mind."

Emily shook her head. "You really do need this personal assistant," she said before giving him a light kiss on the cheek and moving away.

Marcus shook his head. He watched Emily until she disappeared. "Great," he muttered.

He had two headaches coming: his cousin Carlos, and the new personal assistant. He had a strange feeling his entire life was about to be shaken up and he didn't like it one bit.

2

Karalee brought her GMC truck to a quick stop. The traffic was moving at a turtle's speed this morning. She looked at her watch. She couldn't be late. Not on the first day. Impatiently, she tapped her clear polished nails on the steering wheel.

She still felt like she was dreaming. She couldn't believe Summer had gotten her a job so quickly. She was truly thankful and excited. She was going to be the personal assistant of Marcus Tucker. She would have to work at the office on a ninety day probationary period, but if things went well, the job would remain hers.

Summer hadn't told her much about Marcus Tucker other than the fact that he was rich and very good looking. She laughed bitterly. It must be nice being born with a silver spoon in your mouth, she thought. She had never been given anything easily. Her entire life had been one big struggle after another. It had made her develop crocodile skin, and she definitely didn't take crap from anyone. But now she had to humble herself and put a muzzle on her mouth.

She needed and wanted this job. She hadn't worked since the unthinkable had happened her senior year in high school and she'd gone to prison. This was her chance to get back on her feet. She had to move into her own place, get a new car and help her mother when and if she returned too. She wanted to be independent. She wanted to take care of all her financial needs and not have to depend on anyone-especially a man- for anything. She didn't want to let summer down either being she'd gotten this job for her. She wouldn't mess up this chance. She promised herself that no matter what Marcus Tucker or anyone else said or told her to do, she would bite her tongue and just do it.

Karalee let out a growl as she focused back on the jammed traffic. It wasn't even noon and already the June heat was unbearable. She wished she had a horn to blow.

While she waited, she fluffed out her natural curls and smoothed one hand across her business suit that Summer had purchased for her yesterday. The baby blue skirt and matching jacket was both stylish and classy. The three inch pumps with crisscross straps to the ankles complemented the outfit perfectly. She looked in the rear view mirror and smiled. The glow had returned to her cinnamon toned skin. She hadn't looked this happy and sharp in a long time.

She glimpsed her watch again. Panic gripped her. She had exactly five minutes before she would be late and Tucker Insurance was ten minutes away.

Summer had showed her how to get to the building yesterday. She wished now that she had let her drop her off this morning like she'd offered, but she didn't want Summer to over work herself being she had Lupus which sometimes caused her to have arthritis.

Finally traffic began moving and Karalee managed to make it to Tucker Insurance with minutes to spare. She still had to get inside and to the twentieth floor where Mr. Tucker's office was located.

She noticed the up to date cars in the parking lot as she searched for a place to park. Her truck stuck out like a sore thumb. She attempted to hide it out of view, but ended up parking on the outskirts of the parking lot.

Karalee killed the engine. She took a deep breath. Her stomach growled, but she was too nervous to eat. She closed her eyes briefly to collect her thoughts.

As she exited the Truck, she couldn't help but to gawk at the massive Tucker Insurance building.

It was twenty stories high and consisted of two twin towers topped with pyramid-shaped roofs. The towers were connected by a ground level rotunda and an elevated sky bridge. The podium of one of the towers housed Marcus Tucker's office. Her heart fluttered.

Inside the building took her breath away. She gawked at the beautiful marble floors and the stylish furniture in the lobby. It was spacious, and the large glass windows throughout were amazing. Professional clad men and women moved to and fro, and she heard an intercom in the background playing soft music and welcoming all visitors.

She moved to the elevator. She was sweating bullets as she mingled inside with the other professionals.

She would have to meet with Val, the office manager first.

In no time she was on the twentieth floor and had no problem finding the office.

Walking inside, a chocolate skinned woman with glasses and a big mold near her lips moved to her.

"Is there something I can help you with?" the woman asked, focusing on her.

"I have a meeting with Val." Karalee answered, suddenly feeling even more nervous.

"I'm Val."

Karalee extended her hand and introduced herself.

Val quickly looked her over and half shook her hand. "Follow me," she ordered, before turning her back.

Karalee followed her into the massive marketing and advertising department. She was led into an impressive looking office.

Val gestured to the chair in front of her desk. "Have a seat," she ordered.

Karalee sat and tried to relax.

Val gave her some paper work to complete so that she could get a company car and a company credit card. Once they were done, Val went over the company's policies and showed her around the massive marketing and advertising department. She led her into a small office with a desk, phone and file cabinet. "This is your office," she announced.

Karalee's smile was a mile long. She was so happy she felt like break dancing.

By the time they made it back to Val's office, Karalee was sure she was going to love working there, despite Val's callous attitude. Val told her to take a seat again. She gave her a folder.

"I have some important notes inside about Mr. Tucker that you need to familiarize yourself with," Val said. She reclined back in her office chair and stared at her with the same stone face. "Have you ever worked as a personal assistant?"

"No."

"I'm shocked they hired someone with no experience," Val muttered under her breath.

Karalee shot her a stern look. The last thing she needed was this nosey woman, digging into her business. "I can handle the work," she assured her.

Val penned her with a glare. "I must warn you, Mr. Tucker's personal and business life is very hectic and demanding. You'll have to run lots of errands, screen all of his personal and business calls, keep up with his scheduling, and sometimes he may need you after normal working hours. Here's a list of things that must be completed by the end of the day. Daily you will be given a list."

Karalee nodded and briefly studied the long list. She had to do over forty errands that ranged from picking up Mr. Tucker's dry-cleaning to securing tickets for an upcoming NBA game. The majority of the things would have to be done outside of the office, and she would have to drive. She felt overwhelmed but in a good way. She was ready to prove herself to Marcus Tucker.

"When do I get to meet Mr. Tucker?" Karalee asked eagerly.

"Not today," Val smirked at her. "He's going to be tied up with other business."

Karalee was disappointed that she wouldn't get to meet the man she would be working for. But she had too much work to do to focus on it. She had to have a cup of iced tea on Marcus Tucker's desk before he arrived at nine. She moved to the tea machine in the office and proceeded to fix a cup.

"What are you doing?" Val asked, removing her glasses and glaring at her.

"Fixing Mr. Tucker's tea," Karalee answered calmly.

"Obviously, you didn't read the notes I just gave you." Val rolled her neck.

Karalee did not like her attitude. She wanted to tell her to go to hell, but she thought about her mother, the house, car and the independence she would obtain with this job and remained professional.

"I looked them over," Karalee answered, being sure her voice remained neutral.

"Then you should know Mr. Tucker likes his tea from Starbucks," Val shot back with an attitude. "

Karalee bit her tongue so hard she tasted blood. "Can I have the key to the company car?"

"You won't get a company car or company credit card until after I process your paper work." Val returned her gaze back to the documents on her desk. "It could take one week at the most." She looked back at her again, slightly frowning. The mold near her lips seemed to triple in size. "You have transportation, don't you?"

Karalee nodded.

"Then what are you waiting on? Get to work," Val demanded nastily. "You have a half hour to have Mr. Tucker's drinks on his desk." She smirked like she was enjoying seeing her under pressure. "Take it from me; he is one grouchy man without his tea. Especially on Mondays. If you're not back here on time, that would make a very bad first impression. And I'm sure you wouldn't want that on the first day; would you?"

Karalee grabbed her purse and fished inside. "No, I wouldn't," she said smiling and showing the truck keys she'd finally found. She didn't know what was up with Val and her snotty attitude, but she wasn't going to let her discourage her. More importantly, she would not fail or be one of the people who'd caved in under pressure.

She strapped on her purse and moved out of the door. There was a Starbucks on Anderson Road but it was twenty minutes away. Driving her truck would take longer. She didn't know how in the hell she was going to be back before Mr. Tucker arrived, but she was determined to do it.

Fifteen minutes later, Karalee was strolling back into the marketing department.

She was proud of herself and thankful she hadn't gotten a ticket being she had sped to Starbucks. She moved to Marcus Tucker's office. She knocked, praying he hadn't arrived yet. When she heard silence, she entered.

His nicely decorated office took her breath away. She'd only seen offices like this on television and magazines. She looked at his massive glass desk and the executive leather office chair. A large, flat screen television was on the wall and she could see downtown Atlanta from the picture windows.

Hypnotized, she placed the iced tea on the desk and moved to the large windows. The view was amazing!

She turned to leave, but the glass desk caught her attention. She loved the office chair. She wanted to see if the chair was as comfortable as it looked. She knew she shouldn't sit in it, but she could not resist.

The seat was so comfortable, she moaned. Seconds passed before she snapped from her foolishness. Marcus Tucker was due to arrive at any moment. She stood from the seat and headed for the door. Her leg accidently hit the desk and a plant fell, spilling dirt onto the floor.

Ding!

She looked around the office, searching for the sound. It was the elevator. She hadn't noticed Marcus Tucker had a private elevator connected to his office, and it was quickly moving up.

She panicked.

Rushing, she picked up the plant and placed it on the desk. She was thankful the pot was plastic. She saw a closet and raced to it. There was a broom and dust pan. She grabbed it and rushed back to the dirt. Sloppily, she swept it up and headed for the trashcan.

She had to have the mess cleaned and be out of the office before Marcus Tucker arrived. The last thing she wanted was to make a bad first impression or lose her job.

***

Marcus Tucker loathed Monday mornings. In fact it was a rule that no one could disturb him until after he had his cup of iced tea. Most people loved coffee, but he preferred tea to fully wake him. It was his only addiction and he had no intention of breaking it anytime soon. Half asleep, he yawned. He needed to wake completely up. Today, he had to be alert. Models were auditioning for the new Tucker Insurance commercial. They would have to recite the company jingle and wear a bikini being the upcoming commercial would deal with watercraft Insurance and take place on a beach. It was up to him to choose the right women.

Over the years, he and the ad agency had come up with some excellent commercials. Each one was laced with humor and focused on unexpected accidents and how easy it was to get coverage from Tucker Insurance. The commercials always got the viewers complete attention too. More importantly, when it was time to shop for Insurance, their company was the first place most consumers remembered and chose.

Marcus leaned against the cushioned walls of his private elevator. His eyes were so heavy he closed them for a few seconds. The ding from the elevator alerted him that he had arrived at his office. He checked his watch. He had an hour to get things together before the auditions. Afterwards, he had a meeting with the company's Spanish Interpreter about the new Tucker Insurance office that they were opening up in Spain. But first he had to have his tea. Without it, he was no good and very short tempered.

Marcus stepped off the elevator and into his office.

He ran directly into a cloud of dust. "What the hell…" He coughed and used his hand to wave away the grime.

"I'm so sorry, Mr. Tucker," a woman standing in front of him stuttered nervously. "I accidently knocked your plant from the desk."

Marcus snatched off his suit jacket and began shaking away the filth. "Don't worry about it," he grunted, not paying her much attention. He did notice her mile long legs. She was a little over 5'9 in height and judging by that, he knew she was a model.

Pissed, he walked to his desk and threw the jacket on the back of his chair. He pressed the intercom to call Val. He couldn't believe she'd sent the model into his office without informing him or without sending in his key staff. He never held auditions without them present.

"Do you want me to finish cleaning?" the woman asked.

"No," Marcus muttered, rubbing his sore eyes. He adjusted his camcorder and sat in his leather office chair. "Let's just get down to business."

"Of course." The woman smiled nervously. She walked to the chair in front of his desk and sat. "What would you like for me to do?"

"Undress." Marcus ordered. He was about to tell her where the dressing room was, and that they would start the auditions once the key staff arrived, but the woman interrupted him.

"Is this a joke?" she laughed, sitting to the edge of her seat.

Marcus glanced at her before returning his focus back to the camcorder. "No. I'm serious. I need to see your body."

For a few seconds, the woman stared at him like he was crazy. Then she shot out of her seat. "Are you insane?" she asked, her hands trembling.

Surprised by her outburst, Marcus stood slowly from his seat, "Is there a problem?"

"Damn right there is!" The woman gawked at him. "You want me to take off my clothes."

"And? What's the problem?" Marcus asked, completely confused.

"There's no way in hell I'm doing that!"

Shocked, Marcus moved to the front of his desk and stared at her. No woman had ever told him no, especially one who wanted to work for him. He frowned. "My goodness; you act like this is your first time undressing to get a job."

The woman's mouth opened and she glared at him. "For your information; it is. I've never had to take my clothes off to get work, and I never will."

"Well, you're not going to get very far in this business," Marcus said nonchalantly.

The woman looked him up and down in disgust. "So that's how it works? A woman has to undress for you in order to get a job? "

"For this job; Yes. And? What's the problem?" he asked, suddenly aggravated.

She collected her purse. "I'm not undressing for you. I'm out of here."

Marcus gave her a flippant wave. "If you don't want the job there are plenty of women who will do whatever I tell them to do to get it."

The woman's chest heaved as she strapped on her purse. She moved to him, standing eye to eye. "I'm sure there are females who would sacrifice their morals and self respect to get ahead. But I'm not one of them, Mr. Tucker. I'm not selling myself out for this job or any other."

Marcus stuffed his hands into the pockets of his pants. "Okay. So what are you waiting on? Leave." He pointed to the door, wanting the rude woman to go.

"You don't have to tell me twice!" she shouted. "You can take this job and shove it!"

Marcus sighed and shook his head as he watched the woman barge out of his office. She almost knocked Val down as she marched down the hallway. He was so over her. She was a model and behaving as if her body was off limits.

"Unbelievable," he muttered. The only thing he wanted was his tea and now thanks to her, he needed an aspirin too.

"Okay, what just happened?" Val asked, moving into the office looking just as dumbfounded as him.

"That model...she's crazy! She just cursed me out. Can you believe that?"

Val closed her eyes and shook her head. "Mr. Tucker, that wasn't a model. "

"Then who in the hell was she?" he asked, grabbing some napkins to wipe the sweat from his face.

"Karalee?"

"Who's Karalee?"

"Your new personal assistant."

"What?" Marcus lowered his face, feeling totally embarrassed. "Call her back in here," he ordered, breathing heavily.

"She's gone, sir."

Marcus slumped into the chair. "She must think I'm a jerk," he said, closing his eyes.

Val moved beside him and rested a hand on his shoulder. "Don't worry, sir. I'll call her and explain this whole misunderstanding."

"No," Marcus protested. "I'll call. Find her number."

Val looked completely puzzled. She leaned against the chair beside his and stared at him.

"Well, what are you waiting on? And why are you staring at me like that?"

"I just never thought I'd see the day when Marcus Tucker would look so worked up over a woman."

"She just cursed me out, Val," Marcus answered, annoyed.

"I understand that," Val smirked, "but can you explain the fire burning in your eyes." She shook her head. "I've been working here for ten years, and I've never seen you look like this."

Marcus closed his eyes and tried to calm himself as Val exited his office. The truth was: he was shaken to the core. Even though the entire argument had been a big misunderstanding, he'd never had a woman stand their ground with him like Karalee. Usually, women did what he told them even when it went against what they believed in.

His heart continued beating wildly. He hated to admit that he was stimulated and intrigued about the firecracker. She had gotten his complete attention.

He tried to remember how she looked being he hadn't bothered to pay her the least bit of attention when he'd entered the office. The most he recalled were her mile long legs, that sexy voice and those lips...

He shook his head, not knowing what had come over him. He smiled, and then he laughed. Damn, he liked her already.

3

Karalee cussed Marcus Tucker out the entire ride home. She called him every name in the book and then some. How dare he disrespect her like that? And how dare he treat her like some tramp who would sell her body to move up the corporate ladder. She didn't play that. Neither did she like it one bit. He'd made her so mad that holding her tongue had gone completely out of the window.

Karalee squeezed the steering wheel and turned onto her street. She tried to think how she would explain this messy situation to Summer. "I'll just tell her the truth," she muttered. And what was the truth? Marcus Tucker had come on to her and turned her on so much that she'd cursed him out. She let out an aggravated sigh. No man had ever stirred her like that; not even Chris. But when she'd seen his handsome face, and heard his deep voice, heat scorched her body and drenched her panties.

She shook her head. Damn, why did he have to be so nasty and smoking-hot at the same time? He was too fine to be a pervert. He was tall. Real tall. He towered over her and made her feel like a dwarf. His hair was low cut, almost bald. He had eyelashes that women dreamed of and a well trimmed goatee that brought out his square jaw. Just the thought of his unbelievable built body, dipped in peanut butter skin, made her want to spread all 6'3 of him all over her.

She cursed and pulled into the scrub lined driveway. She was relieved Summer wasn't home. She parked her beat up truck and grabbed her purse. She felt entirely disappointed that things had gone this way. She had messed up big time. As she exited through the passenger door, she wondered who in the hell she had pissed off in another life for all these bad things to be happening to her. She was no saint and she could spit fire from her tongue when she was upset, but she had a heart of gold and treated people fair. Even her own mother who was largely responsible for how her life had turned out.

Her cell phone started ringing. She used her hip to slam the passenger door closed. She looked at the caller I.D. It was Summer, the last person on earth she wanted to talk to at the moment. She was tempted to press the end button, but she knew better.

"I'm out running errands," Summer said excitedly. "Why don't I pick you up so we can head over to Lobster World to get something to eat? You can tell me all about how your first day on the job is going while we're there."

Karalee closed her eyes and inhaled sharply. "It didn't go well," she confessed.

"What do you mean?"

"I quit."

"You what?" Summer shouted so loudly Karalee had to move the phone away from her ear.

"Wait," Karalee said. "Give me a chance to explain."

"There's no need to." Summer sounded pissed. I already know what happened. You couldn't hold that tongue of yours, could you?"

"I had good reason not to," Karalee answered.

"And why is that?"

"Marcus Tucker came on to me."

Summer laughed like she'd just heard a funny joke. "Get out of here."

"I'm serious. He's a pervert. He wanted me to undress for him."

"I don't believe you."

"Why would I lie?"

"I worked for The Tucker men for eighteen years before I got sick, and if there's one thing I know: they don't have to ask women to undress; women throw themselves at them. Are you sure you didn't misunderstand what he said?"

"Look, I'm telling you the truth. He's a sick man."

"Where you at?"

"Your place."

"Listen, my phone is going dead," Karalee said, happy that the battery was low. She didn't want to hear her sister's mouth. "We'll talk about this when you get home."

"I'm coming home now," Summer informed her before hanging up.

Karalee's shoulders slumped. The day can't get any worse," she muttered. She unlocked the door and moved inside the house. Her eyes landed directly on Spider. She'd spoken too soon. He was in the kitchen, cutting a man's hair. In her opinion he was really bringing her sister and her beautiful home down.

Karalee shook her head and shut the door.

"Can't speak?" Spider asked.

"That goes both ways." Karalee locked the front door. "You could have spoken first."

"But this my house," Spider shot back.

"Funny; I thought this place belonged to my sister," Karalee placed her keys back inside her purse before focusing on him. "After all, she is the only one working and paying the bills."

Spider stopped trimming the man's head and frowned at her. "I bring in more money then you," he shot back. "All you doing is running up the light and water bill. At least I can give your sister a little change from time to time. What you giving or paying her?"

For the first time Karalee was silent.

"Just like I though; nothing."Spider smirked. "Anyway, what you doing back so early?"

"That's none of your business?" Karalee answered, hating she had to go near Spider, but her cell phone charger was in the cupboard. He stood in front of the cabinet, blocking her.

"Excuse you," she said. He stepped aside and she grabbed the charger. When she turned around Spider was directly in her face. He was a few inches taller than her and the shoulder length dreads in his hair looked like they hadn't been washed in years.

"Can you move?" she asked with an attitude.

Spider inched in closer, trapping her. "Not until we get one thing straight."

"And what's that?"

"I ain't going nowhere."

"Neither am I." Karalee stood her ground. "At least not anytime soon," she muttered, thinking about the job she'd just lost.

"So, for the sake of the woman we both love, why don't we try and get alone," Spider suggested. "Let's put our differences aside and be adults, okay?"

Karalee didn't want to hate the man, and plus she was too exhausted to argue. She took a deep breath and was about to say okay when he reached across her to grab a soda from the refrigerator. His arm brushed over her breasts as he retrieved the drink.

He smiled sneakily and took a swig, focusing his perverted eyes directly on her hips. She knew he'd fondled her breasts on purpose. She remembered how he'd slapped her butt the first day she'd arrived. He'd done that on purpose too. Her skin crawled and she felt sick. Her first impression of him had been accurate. She shook her head and shoved him before storming away. She could still hear Spider laughing as she moved to the basement.

Just the other day, she'd tried to tell Summer to check her man, but she'd brushed the butt slap off. She knew she'd downplay this too. She would have to get her own place and quick.

She slammed the door shut and dropped onto her bed. Her eyes burned with tears. She was back at square one. No job, home, wedding, baby or fiancé and her mother was nowhere to be found. She felt like a guinea pig in a maze. She was trapped. There was no way out. Every time she took a step forward something would happen that would make her take two back.

A tear slipped from her eye. She wished her grandma were still alive. She'd always had the right words to say to make her feel better. She took off her earring and realized that one was missing. Her grandmother had given her the earring before her death and now she'd lost it. Nothing was going right.

Snow white jumped onto her lap and purred. She smiled. She could always depend on her cat who loved her unconditionally.

Karalee thought about how Spider had fondled her breast again. Feeling nasty, she shivered. She stood from the bed and headed to the shower. Summer would be there soon and she wanted to be completely relaxed.

Seconds later, she was under the spray of warm water. Depression tried to set in, but she fought it off. She stepped out of the shower and dried her body with a white, fluffy towel. She slipped into a nightgown and a robe. She had a massive headache and just wanted to sleep her troubles away. Tomorrow things would be better. She would start over. She was a strong woman. Had always been. She'd had no other choice. She refused to quit. She would put in job applications at every restaurant and warehouse in town if it came down to it. She was not staying down. She was determined to be independent and take care of herself and her mother when and if she found her.

Just as she came from the bathroom there was a light tap on the door. "Come in," she said, turning her attention to the perfume on the dresser behind her. She closed her eyes, preparing herself for the argument she knew was sure to take place between her and Summer.

***

Marcus Tucker tried to figure out what in the heck had come over him as he stood outside of the basement door.

A man named Spider had told him he could find Karalee there. He though he'd heard someone on the other side tell him to come in, but he wasn't sure.

Marcus shook his head. What was he doing? Had he lost his mind? He'd never chased after a woman. His breath caught in his chest, and he swallowed the lump in his throat. His massive hands were shaking. He was nervous. No woman had ever made him feel jumpy. Maybe I should have let Val call her, he thought. The entire misunderstanding could have easily been cleared up over the telephone. But the truth was: he wanted to see the firecracker that had cursed him out. She had brought something inside of him back to life.

Marcus knocked on the basement door again. This time he was sure he heard someone on the other side tell him to enter.

He twisted the knob and walked into the basement which looked more like an apartment. What he saw before him made him forget how to speak English.

Karalee had her back to him. She was dress in a short, sexy robe with one of her mile long legs propped up on a chair. He could smell the sweet scent of the perfume she was spraying onto her neck.

Hypnotized, he watched as she moved her leg back to the floor and fluffed out her natural curls. Damn, how could he have not paid her any attention? Was he so hardened by women from the past that he wouldn't notice something different? She was certainly special. Unable to look away, he moved deeper into the room.

"Summer before you go off, please let me explain why I quit that job." Karalee said, talking with her back still to him. "Marcus Tucker is a sick man. He's a freak. A ho."

Marcus snapped from his trance. "I beg your pardon." He held up his index finger. "I'm not a ho."

Karalee jerked around and again he was mesmerized.

Slowly his eyes traced over her face. She was a natural beauty! Everything about her was organic from her hair to her flawless cinnamon toned skin. But it was her almond shaped eyes and the blaze burning in them that held him hostage.

"What are you doing in here?" Karalee asked, quickly tying her robe.

Marcus held up both of his hands to stop her from overreacting. "Spider told me I could find you down here."

"Yeah; but why are you here?" Karalee asked.

"Calm down," Marcus managed to say.

"Calm down?" Her eyes grew wide and her face completely reddened. "I want you to leave! Now!" She rushed past him to the door.

Marcus remained stuck to his spot. "No; Not until I apologize."

Karalee's chest heaved. "You've got that right. You disrespected me."

"I had no intention of disrespecting you," Marcus began explaining. "It was a big misunderstanding."

"Misunderstanding? How so?" Karalee asked, narrowing her eyes.

"I thought you were a model," Marcus explained.

Karalee frowned and then she laughed. "You expect me to believe that?"

"It's the truth." He pulled the paper with the casting information from his pocket and moved to her.

Karalee eyed him suspiciously before she snatched it from him. She studied the paper for few seconds. When she finally met his gaze she looked completely embarrassed.

Marcus took that as his chance to close the space between them. "I hope you'll accept my apology. I would have called, but I felt the need to apologize in person. I'm sorry for this entire misunderstanding."

Karalee stared at him boldly. "Apology accepted. I also want to apologize for my rude behavior. I shouldn't have talked to you the way I did."

Marcus stuffed his hands into his pockets. "Aren't you going to apologize for calling me a freak and a ho?" he asked, with teasing in his tone.

Karalee smiled and it was more beautiful than watching the sun rise.

"Okay; I'm sorry for that as well. I apologize for everything," she said, sounding sincere. "But under the circumstances you've got to understand why I thought that about you."

Marcus nodded. "I do. But I can assure you I've never disrespected a woman and I never will."

"So can we start over?" he asked.

"I don't see why not," Karalee answered.

Marcus extended his hand the way he should have done when he'd first met her. "I'm Marcus Tucker."

"Karalee Johnson," she said, placing her soft hand into his.

A bolt of electricity shot through his flesh. Marcus tried to breathe normally, but the thrilling shocks moving up and down his arms had him breathing like he'd just worked out at his gym. He'd never felt that type of power before and it increased his heart beat to a dangerous speed.

"So, I hope I'll see you at work tomorrow," he said, trying to get his breathing under control.

Karalee looked stunned. "You mean I'm not fired?"

"Of course not. I have a very hectic life and I need a proficient assistant. The job is still yours; that is, if you want it?"

"Are you kidding me?" Karalee laughed and her eyes lit up. "Of course. I'll be there. What time?"

"Eight a.m sharp," he said, laughing at her excitement.

Marcus shook her hand again and proceeded to walk away, but something inside wouldn't let him leave. He wanted to stay and talk with her more. He wanted to dig deeper into her psyche and see what she was about. "Would you mind having lunch with me?"

A tiny frown creased Karalee's brow. "Mr. Tucker, I think we'd better stick to a strictly professional relationship."

Marcus looked deeply into her eyes. "It is strictly professional. I'd just like to get to know my new personal assistant."

Karalee folded her arms across her chest and eyed him suspiciously. "Do you get to know all of your assistants?"

Marcus was shocked by her question. The truth was: none of his other past assistants had caught his attention, but she had and his curiosity was inflamed. He refused to tell her that though. Instead he stuttered all over himself. "Uh, well, no." He leaned on the wall. "I was hoping I could start things off differently with you."

Karalee looked boldly at him. "I'll have to decline."

"Decline?" Marcus asked, unable to mask his shock or disappointment.

"Yes. Refuse, reject, turndown-"

"I know what decline means," Marcus stopped her.

"Then why that look?" Karalee asked, narrowing her eyes.

"What look?"

"Like you've never been turned down before."

"I haven't," Marcus admitted honestly. "At least not from a woman."

Karalee stepped in to him. A smirked teased the corners of her lips. "We'll, I hate to bust your bubble, Mr. Tucker. But this is the real world. You can't get everything you want."

"Is that right?" he asked, enjoying the stare down between them.

"Yeah that is right," Karalee shot back. She opened the basement door. "Besides, they'll be plenty of time for us to get to know each other professionally later," she added, emphasizing the word professionally. "Now, if you'll excuse me, I need to get dressed."

Marcus nodded and walked outside. He wanted to get another good look at the woman who'd told him no twice in one day, but before he could face her, the door shut.

"Very interesting lady," Marcus said, stroking his goatee. She was more than a pretty face and a sexy body. She had a personality that intrigued him. He too was sure that there would be plenty of time for them to get to know each other later. But he had a strange feeling it wouldn't be professionally. He straightened his stylish tie and moved up the basement stairs.

"You expect me to believe that bull?"

Karalee turned from the counter where she'd been preparing a family-pack microwaveable steak and gravy dinner. She'd forgotten Summer was in the kitchen. In fact she'd forgotten about everything, including the steaks and gravy that smelled like it was burning. She pulled it from the microwave, but noticed ice was still in the center. She placed it back inside and set the timer again. Afterwards she searched for the brown rice that she'd forgotten to put on. Now they would have to wait thirty minutes to eat dinner. Not that she had much of a need to eat. Marcus Tucker had taken her appetite alone with her mind.

After he'd walked out of the basement, she hadn't been able to focus on anything but him and his sexy eyes. And by the look in them, he wanted her. But for what? Sex? A one night stand? Of course. A man like that could pick and play over any woman he chose. She wouldn't go out like that. She wasn't a wham bam thank you ma'am type of woman, and she certainly wasn't interested in getting into another relationship. Especially with a man who wasn't committed for the long haul. And a man as fine as Marcus Tucker, was probably not looking to settle down. Falling for him would only lead to trouble and heartbreak. For now, she had to stay focus on her goals and finding her mother.

Still, it was hard to ignore how much Marcus Tucker had turned her on. By the time he'd left the basement, she was so hot she'd had to sit in front of the air conditioner just to cool down. After he'd explained the misunderstanding, her attraction to him had tripled. He really had her twisted inside. She'd only been apart from Chris for a little over two months. But at the moment, Marcus had her feeling weak in the knees whenever he was in her presence. She wondered how she was going to be able to keep her hormones in check while working for him. Just one smile or even the sound of his sexy voice was sure to make her heart forget its natural rhythm.

"Hello; girl, did you hear me?" Summer cut into her thoughts.

Karalee blinked, coming back to reality. She focused on Summer who was sitting at the kitchen table, cutting tomatoes for the salad. "I'm sorry. What were you saying?" she asked, shaking her spinning head.

"You said Marcus Tucker came here, didn't you?

"Yeah."

"And offered you your job back after you cussed him out?"

Karalee nodded.

"That makes no sense," Summer said, placing the knife on the cutting board and staring at her.

Karalee scooped up brown rice and dumped it into the pot. "I don't understand why you find that so hard to believe."

"Well, for one thing," Summer said, sitting forward in her seat. "Marcus Tucker has managers and supervisors deal with his employees. I don't understand why he'd come here to my little old house to apologize to you? Unless-" Summer's words stopped and she shook her head.

"Unless what?" Karalee asked, looking directly at her.

A smile crept up on Summer's face. "Unless he's been struck by cupid's arrow." She laughed.

"That is ridiculous," Karalee squeezed her eyes closed and prayed for her heart to slow its pace. She didn't understand what was happening to her. She wasn't a gullible woman who melted at the sight of a gorgeous, successful man. Chris had fooled her, but she would make sure he was the first and only man to do that.

Still, she couldn't deny that something odd had happened between her and Marcus. When she'd placed her hand into his, every nerve in her body had reacted.

She moved to the sink to cover the brown rice with water. Suddenly, her throat felt parched. She grabbed a cup and filled it. In less than a second she downed the entire thing.

"It was no mistake for you to move back here." Summer had laughter in her voice.

Karalee frowned. "Summer you're being ridiculous. I don't know this man. I don't want to get to know him. I'm just trying to get back on my feet. Don't make nothing into something, okay?"

"Alright. I'll just wait and see what the end is going to be, Karalee Tucker."

Karalee threw the kitchen mitten at her.

"That name does have a ring to it, doesn't it?" Summer continue laughing as she repeated the name Karalee Tucker again.

Karalee shook her head and moved back to the stove with the pot. As she placed the pan on the range, a dreamy smile plastered her face. She got a mental picture of Marcus Tucker's magnificent body. He was a nice, tall drink of water! Even though he'd worn a full suit she'd clearly noticed the man had rock hard biceps, long muscular thighs and a waist that she wanted to wrap her legs around. Piercing pain brought her from her lustful daydream. "Ouch!" she shrieked.

Summer jumped from her chair. "What happened?"

"I burned my hand," Karalee moaned.

Summer turned off the microwave. "You burned the steaks too. How in the hell did you burn a microwave dinner, girl?"

"I'm sorry," Karalee said, feeling terrible that she'd let thoughts of Marcus Tucker mess up a good meal. She cursed her flesh for reacting to him.

"Don't worry about it." Summer moved to the freezer and grabbed some ice cubes. She placed them in a zip lock bag and moved back to Karalee. "I'll just order pizza."

"I hate you have to spend extra money." Karalee shook her head. "I don't know where my brain is at today."

"On Marcus Tucker," Summer said as she pressed the zip lock bag against Karalee's burned fingers. "You were thinking about him, weren't you?" Karalee snatched the bag from her and shook her head in embarrassment. "No...hell no at that."

"Oh really?" Summer asked with a look of disbelief on her face. "Then please explain to me why in the hell you're cooking grits? We were supposed to have brown rice with dinner."

4

Marcus Tucker awoke slowly. He stretched out across his king-sized bed. His eyes remained closed, but the first thing that entered his mind was Karalee. She'd been working as his personal assistant for two weeks, and he was still not able to forget the impression she'd left on him. The fact that she was constantly on his mind troubled him.

However, what bothered him the most was that she'd told him no. Her refusal to break bread with him had plagued his mind since their first meeting. Maybe she has a boyfriend, he thought. That was the only logical explanation as to why she'd refused to have lunch with him. But why did she stay so late at the office, working after everyone else was gone? He worked late too being he had no one to come home to. Maybe she had no one to go home to either.

Thinking he'd overslept, he opened his eyes and sat to the edge of the bed. He looked around the massive bedroom of his home. He'd purchased the 8000-square foot house a year ago. Even though it was beautiful, it was also very lonely. But things had to be this way. Women were nothing but trouble, and a man like him had to be careful who he allowed around him. He was sort of happy now that his cousin would be arriving today. Maybe the young man could keep him company.

He dragged his hands down his face before his eyes rested on the time. It was five minutes to six. Something was wrong. He didn't understand why he'd been waking up so early lately. Usually he slept as late as he could being he went to bed way after midnight.

Now, he wasn't even tired. He felt well rested and more relaxed than ever before, and he didn't need tea to wake him up or energized him anymore. He felt like an excited kid, eager to go on a field trip.

He wondered what had triggered his jubilant mood. He dropped his head. "Karalee." He whispered her name and his heart rate doubled. Karalee was unlike any woman he'd ever encountered. She was stunning, and she smelled amazing! However, it was her mind and personality that had him curious. The fact that she didn't bite her tongue, and refused to worship the ground he walked on, completely turned him on.

Rising from the bed, he noticed his male hood was poking out. He sucked his teeth. He'd had his nature in check for a long time, but Karalee had screwed up his system. His body was reacting to her, and there wasn't a thing he could do to stop it.

He headed for his massive closet. For almost twenty minutes he searched through his suits and shoes, but nothing seemed good enough. He realized then that he wanted to impress Karalee. He wanted her to think he looked good and smelled nice too. He sighed and closed his eyes. He felt foolish for responding to her so quickly. Maybe if she'd gone to lunch with him he wouldn't have felt this way now. Maybe then he would have realized that his theory was true about women only being interested in what he had, instead of who he was as a man.

Still, he'd thought he'd seen something different in her eyes. He'd felt something different with her too. Maybe he was imagining that or just going crazy. He didn't know what was pulling him to her, but he wanted the obsession to past.

Finally he selected his cologne, suit and shoes. It was too early to dress, so he headed for the shower. As the water began cascading down his body, he once again thought about Karalee. She's something else, he thought, unable to stop his smile. He felt his body coming to life again. He hadn't been with a woman in close to a year. But at the moment, she had him rethinking being sexless.

For a few seconds, he thought long and hard about what he had to do to get over this sudden attraction to her. He decided then that she would have lunch with him today. He would put her in a position where she couldn't turn him down. He was sure once they dined, and he found out what she was truly about, the attraction would be a thing of the past. For now, he had to calm his nature. He readjusted the shower knob and turned the water on cold.

***

Marcus looked up from the files on his desk when he saw the tall figure identical to him, standing in his office doorway.

"What's going on this morning?" His brother Jayden asked, entering his office and closing the door.

"Nothing much," Marcus answered, smiling as he pushed his files aside.

"Just working on this paperwork to open the new office in Madrid."

Jayden sat on the office sofa across from him. He took off his glasses which made him look studious. "You nervous?" he asked.

Marcus smiled. Jayden knew him better than anyone. He was a year younger than Marcus, but he was serious, mature and a good listener. Due to that, the two of them had always been very close.

"I think I'm just as nervous as you were the day you became Vice President."

Jayden chuckled and rubbed his massive hands together.

"I've been stressing over this closing for months," Marcus said, dragging a hand across his low cut hair. "The property agent is flying in from Madrid this week. He only speaks Spanish, so that complicates the closing."

"Good thing you have, Alejandro, our company Interpreter," Jayden reminded him.

"Yeah; I just want everything to run smoothly and to close on the scheduled date."

"You'll do fine," Jayden reassured him.

"Anyway, what brings you here?" Marcus gave his brother a curious stare.

"Your new assistant."

"What about her?" Marcus sat at full attention.

"She brought some documents to my office yesterday."

"And?" Marcus asked, trying to figure out where this conversation was headed.

"She's a looker."

"I didn't notice," Marcus said, returning his gaze to the file.

"Get out." Jayden eyed him suspiciously. "Every guy in my department was trying to hit on her."

Marcus didn't understand why he felt a twinge of jealousy, or why he was squeezing the pen in his hand.

"Are you okay?"

"Yes," Marcus answered, retrieving his flies and flipping through them again. "Why?"

"You look a little upset." Jayden smiled and then he laughed. "I can't believe it. She grabbed your attention too, didn't she?"

"Please." Marcus forced a laugh.

"We'll, there's no need to worry, brother."Jayden placed his glasses back on and fixed his colorful bowtie. "She put every one of those men in their places. That woman may be pretty, but she sure has a snappy mouth."

"Don't I know it." Marcus chuckled.

"I'll tell you what," Jayden said, smiling as he stood. "She's not gonna be single for too much longer."

Again, Marcus felt a twinge of jealousy. "And why would you think that?"

"From the look in your eyes, you'll take her off the market."

Marcus balled up a piece of paper and threw it at him. "Please get out of here."

Jayden stood and winked an eye at him. "Alright, I'll go. But I'm warning you. You'd better watch out."

"For what?"

"You may end up like Ford," he said, referring to their brother.

"That will never happen."

"Ford said the same thing and now look at him, married with three kids."

Jayden winked an eye at him and left the office.

Marcus sat back in his chair. He looked at the clock. He'd had enough of this foolishness, it was time to find Karalee and put his plan into action. After lunch, he was sure he wouldn't think about her again.

***

Karalee loved working at Tucker Insurance. Every day she couldn't wait to get to her office. She made sure she stayed on top of her work. Sometimes, she left after everyone else was gone, but she didn't mind. After all the years of not having a job, she was thankful to be working.

This morning, she stepped inside the elevator with a radiant smile. The only person inside was a balding white man, reading the morning paper. She said good morning and moved next to him. She pressed the button for the twentieth floor and inhaled deeply. She hoped and prayed the nerves in her stomach would settle down. But the truth was: she was excited about the possibility of seeing Marcus Tucker. She looked at the cup of tea sitting neatly inside the carryout Starbuck's tray. She'd gotten it on her way to work. She hoped Marcus would be inside his office when she dropped it off.

She didn't get to see him much. Over the last two weeks, she'd only seen him three times when she'd delivered his iced tea. The most they'd said was good morning. But this week, she hoped to see him more. She was still very ashamed about what had happened during their first meeting, but she hoped she could make up for it by doing a proficient job.

The elevator moved slowly up and stopped on the next floor. The balding man stepped off. The door was about to close when a burly woman entered, pushing a janitor cart. She pressed the button for the eighteenth floor before moving beside Karalee and saying good morning.

The woman took a double look at her. "Karalee," she said, staring at her.

Karalee looked her over. "Do I know you?"

"It's me, Wanda…big Wanda."

Karalee felt her heart drop into her stomach. This was not happening today. Of all the people she could have run into, why did it have to be big Wanda? Big Wanda knew too much about her and her past. She'd used to live across the street from her grandmother and had been privy to a lot of their personal business.

"Girl, you look good!" Wanda said, talking loudly. "I haven't seen you-"

"Since I went to prison," Karalee finished the sentenced for her.

"That's right. What you doing here?"

"I work here."

"Ain't that a trip?" Wanda laughed, revealing a gold front tooth. "Me too. I'm a janitor."

"Which department you work in?"

"Marketing."

"Oh snap, girl. You done moved up," Wanda laughed, shoving her shoulder.

Karalee held on tightly to the drink and tried to smile so her annoyance wouldn't show.

Wanda looked her over slowly. "I'm glad to see you doing good, girl. How's your mama?"

"Alright; I guess."

Wanda shook her head. "I tell you what: you did good by your mama after your grandma died. When you went to prison, I was upset. It's a shame what happened."

The elevator stopped on another floor. The doors opened and Val walked in.

Karalee felt as if her heart had stopped beating. The last thing she needed was for Wanda to keep running her mouth, and for Val to find out she'd been in prison. Her mean ass would really play that out.

"Hey, let me get your number so we can hang out," Wanda kept talking.

Karalee pulled out her cell phone and the two exchanged numbers.

"This my stop." Wanda smiled. "It was good running into you. I'll call you later, alright?"

"Yeah, sure," Karalee said, hoping she'd get the hell out of the elevator.

The door closed and Karalee breathed a sigh of relief.

Val didn't say anything, not even good morning, but Karalee noticed the curious look on her face.

When the elevator arrived on their floor, Karalee took a deep breath and stepped off behind Val. She was about to head to her office, but Val ordered her to come to her workplace.

Val closed the door and placed a folder on her desk. "Here's today's work."

Karalee placed the Starbucks tray on the small table. She picked up the folder and looked over the list. There were over eighty things that needed to be done. She met Val's evil gaze and took a deep breath to get a hold of her emotions. "Val," she said as calmly as possible. "There is no way I can do all of these things today."

Val inched in so close she could see the hairs coming out of the mold near her lips. "See that it gets done before five." She smirked. "Or someone else will gladly do it for you." She walked away, closing the office door behind her.

Karalee shook her head and slammed the folder down on the desk. She was beginning to think Val was an evil witch. She was sure if she threw water on her, she would melt and go up in smoke. She couldn't understand how someone could be so mean. The lady had some serious issues. She was not going to go there with her, or do anything to get fired. That's exactly what Val wanted. "God, you know how much I need this job." She picked up the tray and looked up to the ceiling. "Please give me the strength and will power…"

There was a knock at the door.

"To resist this man," Karalee mumbled when she eyed Marcus Tucker strolling inside. As she digested his 6'3, ripped physique, she forgot how to breathe. His juicy lips were moving and she was sure he was saying something, but the only sound she could hear was her pounding heart. Her hands weakened. Afraid she'd drop the tray, she placed it back on the desk.

Marcus moved before her. When he said good morning she snapped from her spell. She shook her dizzy head and managed a wobbly smile.

"Good morning back to you," she greeted, trying to remain calm. "If you're looking for Val, she just stepped out."

"I didn't come here for Val." Marcus cut her off. His eyes lowered, devouring her from head to toe. "I want you."

Chills ran down Karalee's spine, but she managed to cock a brow. "You want me?" She repeated unsure of what he met, or why he'd said it in such a low, sexy tone.

Marcus shook his head. "Y-Yes," he stuttered and cleared his throat while searching for the right words. "I need you to work alongside me today."

Karalee tried not to grin as he laughed nervously.

"Is it hot in here or is it just me?" he asked, wiping sweat from his brow.

Karalee shrugged. "It feels fine to me."

"We'll, I'm burning up." He loosened his tie and pointed to the tray. "Is that iced tea for me?"

Karalee nodded, trying her hardest not to laugh as he leaned in to retrieve the drink. The smile instantly faded when his juicy lips connected to the cup. It was the sexiest thing she'd ever seen. Unexpectedly, her nipples hardened and her crotch began throbbing. She found herself staring and wishing she could trade places with the mug for just a few seconds.

She cursed silently. What in the hell is happening to me? She wasn't the type of woman to melt over a man. But Marcus Tucker was the word sexy in the flesh, and he smelled like a dream. Still, she was determined not to let her raging hormones control her or make her lose focus on her goals.

"What sort of work do you want me to do, Mr. Tucker?" Karalee asked, once he lowered the cup from his succulent lips.

"I need your help with auditions," he said, appearing to regain his composure.

Clearing her parched throat, Karalee picked up the file. "What am I supposed to do about the work Val gave me today? She said it had to done before five."

Marcus stepped in close and peered at her with his hypnotic eyes. Her legs threatened to buckle as he took the folder.

"Don't worry; I'll handle Val."

She let out a relived breath when he stepped to the door.

"Ladies first," he said, waiting for her.

On weak knees, Karalee walked out of the office. She wondered how in the heck she would make it through the day with this irresistible man.

***

Marcus snuck a peek at his Rolex. The saying, a watched clock never moved, was true. He'd been glimpsing the time and waiting for noon all morning. Now, it had finally arrived.

Marcus looked at Karalee for what had to be the hundredth time. He was supposed to be observing the models that were sashaying in and out of his office, but he couldn't keep his eyes off of her. She was like spring, and her presence had brought him from a deep hibernation. He was ready to satisfy his appetite- an appetite that had been suppressed for way too long.

Marcus dragged his manicured hand down his face, not understanding what had come over him. He'd been around the world and had met some very interesting people in his lifetime, but none had high jacked his mind like Karalee. He hoped that once he had lunch with her, he could get back to being the old Marcus.

"Mr. Tucker?"

Realizing someone was speaking to him, Marcus shook his head. It was one of the models. "Uh… yes," he said, sitting up and clearing his throat.

"Do you need me to do anything else?"

"No, I believe we're done. Right?" he asked his key staff which consisted of ten people.

They all nodded in approval and Marcus announced it was time for lunch. Anxiously, he gathered his files and searched the room for Karalee. She was nowhere in sight. Just as he was about to go search for her, he felt a tap on his shoulder. He turned. Immediately his hormones went into over drive when he realized it was Karalee. He tried not to stare, but for the first time he noticed the color of her eyes. They were chestnut brown and seductive. Beautiful!

"Is there anything else you'd like me to do?" She asked, giving him the audition sheets.

"How about lunch?"

"Sure; do you want me to order for you?" Karalee offered.

"Actually, I already did."

There was a knock on the door, followed by a man bringing in boxes of takeout.

As the man placed the food on the table, Karalee looked completely puzzled.

"Before you say anything, I need you to work through lunch so I took the liberty to order for the both of us."

"Well, I wish you would have told me earlier," Karalee said, making her way to the corner and lifting her large purse. "I brought my own lunch."

He stared at her in disbelief. "So, you're going to let me eat all of this food by myself?"

She cocked a brow. "Thanks for the kind gesture, but I'm good."

She pulled out her lunch bag. "I have peanut butter and..." Her words came to a sudden halt, and she immediately dropped the bag to the floor. Ants were all over it.

"Don't touch it!" he warned. In the flash of an eye, he had the lunch in a tied trash bag and outside of his office door, ready for maintenance pick up.

Karalee looked completely embarrassed as she finished cleaning out her purse. Both moved to the sink and washed their hands.

"The ants must have gotten into my purse this morning when I had it in my truck," Karalee said, throwing her towel in the trash.

Marcus washed and dried his hands. "So I guess that means you can have lunch with me now, right?"

Karalee's mouth parted on the verge of reply, but a loud growl came from her abdomen, stopping her.

Marcus bit back a laugh. "Was that a yes I heard from your stomach?"

Karalee closed her eyes briefly. "I guess I am a little hungry," she admitted.

"A little hungry?" he laughed. "It sounds like world war one is going on inside your stomach."

Karalee smiled, showing her sparkling teeth. The site was so hypnotizing his heart began beating at a dangerous speed. He took a deep breath to calm himself. "Well, what are you waiting on?" he asked, heading for the table. "Let's eat."

He pulled out her chair. After she was seated, he leaned in to help her push it closer to the table. "I hope you like Chinese," he said, his mouth close to her ear.

She looked up. They were eye to eye and almost lip to lip.

"I actually love Chinese," she answered in a sexy tone.

Immediately his temperature began rising, along with the tent in his pants. "Me too." He gave her a box and a drink." I guess we'd better eat before it gets cold." Swiftly, he moved to his seat, hoping she wouldn't notice his arousal. When he sat, he was relieved to see she was fully focused on her meal.

Marcus briefly closed his eyes. My plan isn't going so well, he thought. Already they had liking the same food in common, and the chemistry was unbelievable.

"So what are we working on?" Karalee asked, interrupting him from his thoughts.

He gave her the files.

As she took it, an earring fell from the folder and landed on the table.

"I've been looking all over for this," Karalee said, looking shocked as she picked up the jewelry.

Marcus leaned forward and stared at her. "I found it in my office chair. I don't know how it got in that file anymore than I know what it was doing in my office chair."

Karalee closed her eyes briefly. "I have a confession.

"A confession?" He looked puzzled.

"Yes; I dropped it when I sat at your desk," she admitted, focusing back on him.

"You sat in my chair?" he asked, thinking she had some nerve.

She looked worried and embarrassed. "Yes, the first day I started work. I'm very, very sorry."

Marcus held up his hand. Anyone else who'd done such a thing would have been reprimanded, but her honesty really impressed him. "It's okay." He assured her. "I used to do the same thing when I was a little boy and my dad would leave me in his office."

She smiled and the tension drained from her face "I just wanted to see how it felt."

"To what? Run a colossal company?"

"No. To pretend that I'd acquired this kind of office by my own blood, sweat and tears.

Marcus was impressed again. It was refreshing to be around an Independent female who wanted to do things on her own. Most of the women from his past had wanted his fame and money to support them. He wiped his mouth and looked at her. "Well, you certainly have the potential to head a department and have an office like this someday." He encouraged her. "You're inquisitive and bold. That's essential to running a business." He twirled up a forkful of noodles and peered at her. "So tell me, where does your bold nature come from?"

Hesitation clouded her gaze.

"Am I getting too personal?"

"Very."

He chuckled.

"But in this case, I don't mind revealing it." She leaned forward and looked at him. "When I was a little girl I had to raise myself and my younger sister. I didn't have time to be a chicken."

"The same here," Marcus said, picking over his food. "My mother died when I was young. A lot of responsibility was placed on me being I was the oldest."

Sympathy flashed in her eyes, and she quickly told him she was sorry. He wanted to ask her if her mother had died too. From the look in her eyes it appeared she had. But he bit his tongue. For now he wanted to find out more about her.

They eased into a smooth conversation from there. Although she shifted it back to complete business, he still enjoyed talking to her.

The more she chatted, the more he realized that he loved the way her mind worked. He'd been searching for a reason not to like her, but they had more in common than he'd thought. And she was not only bold and beautiful, but very smart. She was also very honest with him when he shared his future advertisement ideas.

Before he realized it, lunch and the afternoon had wasted away and the evening sun was shining through his office windows. They ended up at his desk going over marketing strategies and sipping iced tea.

"Before you leave, let me show you one of our print ads," he said, grabbing the newspaper. "I really liked some of your ideas and would love your opinion."

"I'd be glad to offer my thoughts," Karalee said humbly. She pulled her chair closer to his.

He opened the paper and turned to the company's page length advertisement. "So what do you think?" He asked, pushing the paper under her nose.

Karalee studied the ad for a few seconds before she spoke. "Your idea to have beautiful female models in your advertisement is great," she complimented. "It will certainly get the male consumers attention, but you do need to mix some hunky men in your advertisement to satisfy the ladies. After all, women account for a large percentage of the decision making regarding most household and insurance purchases. You need to grab their attention too."

He turned to her. "And what type of hunky guys do you suggest?" he asked, wanting to know what sort of men she found attractive.

"Richard Gere and Tyson Beckford aren't so bad," she joked.

They both laughed. Marcus hadn't laughed this much in a long time and it felt good. Too good. "Well, those guys are out of the question," he said, flipping to the next page. He pointed to a male clothing model. "What about this guy? Will he do?"

Karalee gave him a flippant wave. "Nah, he's cute, but we need a male who can snatch a woman's complete attention."

He picked up the paper and flipped through it again, studying more males. Then he lowered the paper some and looked at her. "I think I've found the perfect guy," he said, smiling.

"Let me see." she demanded playfully.

He placed the newspaper on the desk and pointed to the new movie star he'd been hearing buzz about. "What about him? He's certainly the type of man women would take a second look at."

Instantly the smile vanished from Karalee's face. Her eyes flashed with anger and hurt as she glared at the article. He thought he saw tears welling up in the corners of her sockets.

She stood abruptly. "I think I'd better be going." She grabbed her purse. "I have tons of other work to do for you."

He was about to ask her if she was okay, but Val moved inside his office.

"Mr. Tucker..." Val stopped in her tracks. She looked from him to Karalee with a surprised look etched on her face.

"Is there something I can do for you, Val?" he asked, feeling annoyed.

"You're sister Emily is expecting you for the five o'clock meeting in the main conference room." She walked to the desk and placed a folder on it. "And Alejandro wants you to look over these papers that he translated from Spanish to English."

Marcus noticed Karalee exiting the office. He wanted to call her back and talk with her more.

"Mr. Tucker."

He pulled his eyes away from Karalee and focused back on Val who he'd completely blocked out.

"What?" he almost shouted.

"It's ten minutes after five," she said, looking at him suspiciously. "You know Emily hates waiting."

I'm aware of the time, Val." He looked for Karalee again, but she was gone. "I'll be ready in a minute." He dropped his gaze back to the newspaper.

Val shook her head and left.

A few minutes later, Marcus grabbed his suit jacket and slid it on. He straightened his tie and headed for his private elevator. He knew he should focus on the meeting, but all he could think about was Karalee. He wondered why the article had upset her so.

5

Karalee was still fuming as she tried to start her truck. She'd been trying to start it for the last hour. "Come on baby. Don't you dare do this to me." She felt tears stinging her eyes, but she refused to let one fall. What a day, she thought. First she'd bumped into Wanda, then she'd seen the picture of her ex fiancé Chris hugged up with his agent in the newspaper, and now her truck wouldn't start. The picture flashed before her eyes again. Her heart began pounding so hard her chest ached. She couldn't believe Chris was getting married to his agent, Brenda. Plus he'd landed the lead role in the upcoming movie, Temptation.

Frustrated and angry, she hit the steering wheel. So many questions moved through her brain she felt dizzy. Suddenly, everything about why Chris left her became crystal clear. He'd been cheating with his agent all the time.

"Bastard," she muttered. She didn't understand how the man who'd she'd been with since sixteen could betray her in such a way. She had supported him when he'd decided to chase his dreams to become an actor. She'd never had money to offer, but she'd given him emotional support and encouragement. Now he was at the top and about to marry his agent. Defeated, she placed her head on the steering wheel. No tears fell, only anger consumed her.

Knock. Knock. Knock.

Karalee jerked her head up. Marcus stood in view. Quickly, she pulled herself together and sat completely up.

"Are you okay out here?"

"I'm fine," she assured him. Karalee plastered on a forced smile and tried to start her truck. It started and she breathed a sigh of relief. "See you tomorrow," she said, waving goodbye as the truck took off. The last thing she needed was for Marcus to be in her personal business. He already knew she was living in the basement of her sister's home. Plus, he'd asked too many questions during lunch, trying to figure her out. Unexpectedly, the truck jerked and a cloud of smoke shot out of the tailpipe. The truck rolled to a complete halt. She tried to start it again, but to no avail.

She couldn't believe her luck. Nothing was going her way today. A few seconds later, there was a knock on her window again.

Marcus bent down and peered at her.

"It doesn't look like you're going anyplace no time soon."

She moved out of the truck through the passenger door and made her way to Marcus at the front of the vehicle.

He chuckled and hit the hood. "This old thing has met its end."

"Well, this old thing has been with me since I was seventeen," Karalee said offended. "It belonged to my grandmother. And unlike people, it never let me down…until now." She cast her eyes away. It seemed like she lost everything she loved.

Marcus held up his hand. I didn't mean to insult your truck. I still have old things that belonged to my mother. People think they are useless, but I know the value."

Their eyes met and held, and Karalee felt the same electric connection that she'd fought off inside his office. She noticed the sad look in his eyes again that had been present earlier when he'd spoken of his mother and siblings too. She was tempted to probe, but decided to keep it professional. However, keeping it professional was getting harder by the second.

"Let me call a tow truck and take you home," he offered.

Karalee snapped from her trance. "I can't afford a tow truck." She looked away, feeling embarrassed.

"Don't worry; I'll take care of it."

Karalee held up a hand. "Look, I don't let people do things for me for free."

Marcus shook his head. "Pride is useless. You can't eat it, wear it or spend it."

Karalee's face tightened. "True," she agreed. "But sometimes it's the only thing I have left."

Marcus stared at her curiously for a few seconds before speaking. "I'll tell you what; why don't I pay for everything. You can work for me on the weekends to pay me back."

"Here?" she asked.

"No, I work with young men at a gym. I could use some extra help."

"And I need my truck fixed." Karalee quickly agreed.

"Then it's settled," Marcus whipped out his cell. "You can start this weekend," he said, dialing the tow truck company.

While they waited, Marcus gave Karalee the address to his gym and helped her get the things from her truck.

In no time her vehicle was hitched up, and she was watching sadly as it was pulled away.

"I'll be back in a second," Marcus said, heading off.

Karalee watched him disappear. It seemed the more she tried to keep her distance, the more things happened to bring them closer together. She didn't understand it one bit. Neither did she understand why she liked it. She was confused. She was trying to get over the sting of one man's betrayal and fighting her attraction to another.

A few minutes later, she heard the roaring of an engine and inhaled the subtle scent of motor oil. She noticed a chromed out Harley Davidson motorcycle heading in her direction. It was Marcus! Slowly, her gaze slid over his 6'3 chiseled body. Damn, he was tall.

And built.

And his feet were big.

Real big.

Instantly, dirty images of him pleasuring her with something the same length as those feet filled her mind. She became so heated she had to fan her face. Just stop it, she warned herself.

Marcus stopped in front of her.

He took off his helmet and flashed that smile that put the sex in sexy. "Hop on," he said, patting the space behind him.

Feeling light headed, Karalee took a deep breath. "Are you serious?" She placed a sweaty hand on her hip. "I thought you were going to give me a ride in your car?"

"I would have, but the weather was nice so I rode my bike in this morning." He frowned. "Don't tell me you're scared." He started clucking like a chicken.

Karalee couldn't help but to laugh. "I'm not a chicken," she said, her pride kicking in. But the truth was she was petrified and it had nothing to do with the bike. The fact that she would be so close to his amazing body instantly made her nipples hard and her panties damp.

"So what are you waiting on?" Marcus asked.

Karalee sucked air into her lungs. She hopped on, trying to stay as far away from his body as possible.

Marcus looked back at her and smiled slyly as she placed on her helmet. "I'm afraid you're going to have to get a little bit closer than that. "

"Closer?" she squeaked.

"Yes." Gently, he yanked her to him and wrapped her arms around his waist.

"Much better," he said with laughter in his tone.

Karalee felt the steel of his abdomen, along with the heat of his buttocks and instantly her crotch began thumping.

"Don't be afraid," he said, soothingly. He stroked her hand. "You're safe with me."

For some strange reason Karalee did feel safe. She'd sensed the nurturing part of him earlier. She had no doubt that he would protect her to the fullest. Still, she resisted falling for him. She was determined to stay in control.

"Speaking of safe," she said, regaining a little power, "How many accidents have you had on this bike?"

Marcus put on his helmet and revved up the engine. "Only three."

"Only three? What the hell-" Before she could finish protesting, the bike took off. Her voice was lost in the wind as her body pressed closer than close to his.

This feels so right, Marcus couldn't help but to think as his bike glided smoothly down the highway. He'd made it his mission to pick Karalee's brain and find out what she was truly about. Now he knew he was in trouble. She was not what he'd expected, and she certainly wasn't like the other leeches who'd only been interested in what he could offer. She was a beautiful, strong and an unpredictable lady who he wanted to get to know better.

However, she was determined to keep it business. Breaking into her would be more difficult than breaking into the White House, but he was up for the challenge. That was the main reason why he'd offered her weekend work. He wanted to be around her as much as possible. He hadn't felt this curious and alive in a while. It felt good.

He was sad when he pulled into her driveway. He'd loved the way her body felt pressed close to his. He shut off the engine.

Karalee hopped off the bike. He moved beside her.

"Thank you for the ride," she said, gathering her belongings.

He held up his hand to halt her. "No need to thank me. I'll pick you up seven-thirty in the morning if you like. I'll drive my car next time."

He noticed the look of uncertainty on her face, and he was sure she would say no. But to his shock, she agreed. He moved next to her. "Can I ask you something?"

"Go on."

"What did you mean when you said: unlike people your truck never let you down"?

"It's personal," she said, quickly trying to shut off the conversation.

Marcus stroked his chin and stared at her. "It wouldn't have anything to do with your boyfriend that I read about in the newspaper today, would it?"

She gasped. "How did you know that?"

"I didn't get this far in business based on luck, and besides, your face told the entire story. What happened?"

Karalee looked hesitant, but to his surprise she answered. "He left me when I needed him the most." He saw pain flash in her eyes, but she quickly recovered.

He wanted to reach out and touch or hug her, and tell her that he too had been with someone who'd left him at his lowest point. But he knew better. Now just wasn't the right time. Instead he slid in closer. "Well, your ex is truly a fool."

Karalee narrowed her eyes and turned completely toward him. "Why do you say that? You don't know me."

"True; but from the little that I do know you seem like a stand up woman." He shoved his massive hands into his slacks and shook his head. "Believe me; they're very rare to come across these days."

Karalee cocked her head sideways and folded her arms across her chest. "Oh, I find it hard to believe that you'd have issues finding a stand up woman."

"Look who's getting personal now," Marcus teased, touching her hand as they both laugh. The electricity returned and he felt his body reacting to her.

Karalee shook her head. "I'm sorry. I shouldn't have said that."

"No, it's okay. Listen, you are my personal assistance. We're going to be around each other a lot. Even more since you'll be working for me on the weekends. So we might as well get to know each other."

He was about to say something else when a beautiful milk white cat came trotting down the driveway distracting him.

Marcus loved animals. From the time he could walk he'd been collecting stray ones and bringing them home. But after his mother died, his life had changed and he wasn't allowed to have them. The cat stopped right at him and he bent to pick it up.

"Don't touch her!" Karalee protested, but he'd already had the cat in his arms, stroking her silky fur.

Karalee appeared shock. "I can't believe it."

"What's wrong?" he asked as the cat snuggled closer to him and purred.

Karalee looked dumbfounded. "Snow White never lets anyone touch her. She has a bad habit of scratching people."

"Well, animals love me." Marcus placed Snow White back on the ground. The cat circled him, pressing her fur against his legs like she was marking her territory.

"I don't know what's gotten into her," Karalee said, looking confused as Snow White went trotting away.

"I guess I'm cat approved," Marcus teased.

"One hundred percent accepted," Karalee said, still shaking her head.

Marcus rubbed his massive hands together. A slight smile made its way across his face. "You know, the funny thing about animals is that they can detect the good and bad in people. Humans have the same ability, but we just don't use or trust it."

Marcus winked an eye at her and said goodbye. He moved to his bike and hopped on. In no time he was speeding away. He hoped she'd gotten the message he was trying to convey. After years of closing off his heart, she had opened it again to the possibility of romance.

6

Marcus gave his cousin a long, tight hug and dab. He pulled away and looked the young man over. His cousin was the splitting image of him with his smooth skin the color of peanut butter, big brown eyes, high cheekbones and long limbs. The only difference was his hair which was done in a baby dreads.

"How was your flight?" Marcus asked.

"It was banging, cuz." Carlos smiled. "I love the private jet."

"I know you do." Marcus smirked as he watched the attendants hurry ahead of them with Carlos's luggage.

Carlos pulled out his touch screen phone, flipping through it. "Hey, thanks for letting me stay with you. After mom died pops started tripping."

"You don't have to explain anything to me," Marcus said, remembering his own childhood and how bad it had been. He promised himself then that he was going to do everything within his power to be there for his cousin the way his father hadn't been there for him.

"Boy, you almost as tall as me," Marcus quickly changed the topic as he looked him over again.

"I am taller than you." Carlos punched Marcus in the chest playfully. "But I wish I had your muscles. You swole, cuz. What do I have to do to get my body to look like yours?"

"Why do you want a body like mines?" Marcus frowned.

"Do you see the way these honies in here are staring at you?"

Marcus shook his head. "This body comes from working out at my gym.

"You still teach boxing?"

"I'm teaching boxing as a way to release stress," he clarified.

"Well, I got a lot of steam I need to blow off. I want to get my body right for the ladies and for the football field." Carlos turned his cap backwards and eyed a young woman who was walking next to him.

Marcus shook his head. His cousin was just as girl crazy as he'd been at that age. He ordered Carlos to pull his pants up as they walked out of the airport.

"Hey, you trying to kill my game, cuz."

"Game?"

"Yeah, this the style. Don't have me looking like Steve Urkel up in here."

"Forget the style," Marcus told him. "You are wearing a belt from here on out. You are a Tucker and-"

"I know," Carlos interrupted as he blocked a playful punch Marcus tried to land to his arm.

Carlos stopped in front of the SUV. "Can we take some pictures?"

Marcus agreed and Carlos positioned the camera phone before them. "These pics are the bomb," he said, flipping through his phone again. "I gotta post these to Face book, twitter and Instagram."

Marcus dragged a hand down his face. He knew having a teenager around was going to take some getting used to. The two entered his vehicle and waited for the baggage to be loaded.

"I've already enrolled you in a private academy for the rest of the summer," Marcus said.

"Cool," Carlos answered while changing the radio to a station Marcus didn't particularly care for. "I sure hope some fine ladies are at this school."

"It's an all male academy."

"What?" Carlos stopped and gawked at him.

Marcus laughed. "Just kidding. But seriously, are women all you think about?"

"Pretty much," Carlos smiled, "along with playing football, clothes, shoes and food. Speaking of food, I'm starving."

"I have plenty of food at my place."

The luggage was loaded and Marcus drove off, mingling with traffic.

"So who you dating now, cuz? The last time I visited you had a fine dime with killer curves."

"Well, I'm single now," Marcus said sourly.

"You kidding me, right? With all these fine honies in ATL." Carlos waved to a group of young girls in a jeep next to them before looking back at him. "What happened?"

"Trouble," Marcus answered, keeping his eyes focused on the road.

"So you don't got nobody?"

Marcus thought about Karalee then and how amazing she'd made him feel today. The thought of how her body felt wrapped around him on the motorcycle made his nature twitch. She was an interesting woman and he couldn't wait until tomorrow to see her. A slight smile creased his face and for a moment, he forgot Carlos was with him.

"You holding out," Carlos laughed. "Some honey got you cheesing like that."

Marcus shook his head and tried to fight off the smile. "Hey, we're talking about you," he said changing the station back to the one he loved. "You have to get settled in. Forget about the ladies. For now anyway," Marcus advised. "I promise they'll be plenty of time for them later."

"Aren't you just like a woman," Karalee scolded Snow White the next morning as she dressed for work.

"Time you see a good looking man you come switching and showing your tail."

Karalee lay on the bed and looked at the ceiling. She let out a long sigh and peered at Snow White who was next to her, licking her paws. "You do have good taste," she almost moaned.

There was no denying that all 6'3 of Marcus Tucker was simply delicious, and his personality was addictive. Plus, they seemed to have a lot in common. She couldn't deny the chemistry between them.

She flexed her fingers. She could still feel the ripples of his washboard stomach and smell his woodsy cologne. She squeezed her legs tightly together and licked her lips. Her body craved him more than the sweetest chocolate, but her mind warned her to keep her distance.

There was no way she would fall head over heels for a man after the way Chris had kicked her heart in the dumpster. She was too fragile, and she wasn't sure of Marcus Tucker's intentions. She couldn't understand for the life of her why a man as fine and successful as him had taken an interest in her. She thought she was pretty, but in no way did she feel like she could compete with the pencil thin, leggy models that had been strutting in and out of his office yesterday.

She stood from the bed and moved to the dresser to retrieve her earrings from the jewelry box. She was happy she'd found the missing one. As she placed it safely back into the box, she noticed the engagement ring Chris had given her. She wondered why she'd held on to it for so long. Especially when she was in this terrible financial situation. She could easily get a good amount of cash for it.

She hated to admit that she'd thought he would return someday and beg her back. Now she knew that would never happen, and she also knew she would never take him back. The picture of him and his agent Brenda smiling happily in the newspaper from the day before swirled through her mind. "Never again," she vowed. She was done with him. It was time to move forward and achieve her goals. The last thing she needed was Marcus Tucker distracting her from doing that.

The ringing of her cell phone grabbed her attention. Picking up the blackberry, she noticed it was Marcus. Her heart jumped into her throat. It was a little after seven. She didn't understand why she was so happy or why her heart was in her throat.

She answered on the third ring. The sound of his raspy voice saying good morning caused her temperature to rise and her tummy to quiver. "Are you ready?"

Weak, she sat on the bed. "Yes," she said, searching the room for her shoes.

"Great; I'll be there in about ten minutes."

Karalee disconnected the phone and quickly finished putting on her last minute things. She was glad she had gotten dressed early. By the time she walked into the living room, a shiny charcoaled black SUV was parked in front of the house.

"Dang girl!" Summer said, closing the shade she was peeping out of. "You've been working for Mr. Tucker for three weeks and already he's brought you lunch, given you a ride on his motorcycle, offered you work on the weekends and now he's picking you up for work this morning too. That man is really feeling you."

Karalee looked in the wall mirror and fluffed out her hair. "Well, he can feel me all he wants to." She grabbed her purse and strapped it on. "I'm here to do a job, not get to know him."

She tried to move away, but Summer stopped her by grabbing her arm. "Girl, what's wrong with you? Why are you being so cold when Mr. Tucker is going out of his way to help you?"

"Look; I don't want some man I hardly know doing things for me."

" Girl, you'd better get off that high horse you riding on and swallow your pride. Have you forgotten you don't have a car?" Summer squeezed her arm tighter. "You don't have anything. You'd better loosen up and get to know that man. He wants to help you and you'd better let him. You should be grateful Marcus wants to make sure you have transportation to work."

Karalee folded her arms defensively across her chest. "Ask yourself some questions. Why is he doing all of this? A man of that Caliber should be dating one of those models that were in his office yesterday, or sailing on his yacht, not worrying about me or trying to figure me out."

"Girl, I swear sometimes you can't see the forest because of the trees."

Karalee rolled her eyes heavenward. "I don't have time for your riddles this morning."

"Well, like it or not you're listening," Summer argued. "Now I know you want to be independent and get everything on your own. After what Chris did, I don't blame you for feeling that way. But I have news for you: nobody can be totally independent. We are living in the real world and everything is based on extended credit." She looked at her watch. "And speaking of extended credit, I need to go to the bank."

Marcus sounded the horn, and Karalee waved outside to let him know she was coming.

"Why are you going to the bank?" Karalee probed.

"I'm short this month on the bills."

"How much?"

"Too much. Anyway I'm taking out a second mortgage on the house, so I'll be alright."

Karalee suddenly felt guilty. She felt bad and wanted to help her sister. "Don't take out a second mortgage."

"I have to." Summer lowered her eyes. "The collection companies are calling and making threats."

"I think I may be able to help."

Summer frowned. "How are you going to help me?"

"Don't worry about that." Karalee grabbed her hand and squeezed it.

Summer looked confused, but she nodded and walked away.

Quickly, Karalee moved back to the basement.

She felt foolish. Her sister was struggling to pay her bills and she was refusing help all because of what Chris had done. Summer was right. She had to let her defenses down and get to know Marcus.

She opened her jewelry box and pulled out the engagement ring. She knew what she had to do.

***

Marcus felt his heart beating out of his neck as he watched Karalee stroll out of her house. For a moment he could not move, neither did he want to. Not only was the woman on point in the brains department, and the most interesting female he'd ever met, but she was also very attractive. He still could not believe he had not noticed her beauty during their first encounter. Bitterness had almost blinded him. He was glad she had snatched his respect and attention in the way she had or he would have not paid her the least bit of mind and labeled her along with the rest. But she was far different from the rest of the women he'd dated or encountered in the past. The woman was a natural beauty. She had a glow to her cinnamon toned skin that made her stand out from the crowd. Her legs were long and shapely. Her naturally curly hair framed her face and brought out her high cheekbones. And those lips...

He shook his head. How he loved her lips. Last night, he had imagined that luscious mouth trailing sweet kisses down his body as he called out her name.

He blinked, pulling himself together. He didn't want to offend her by gawking at her like some pervert, but he couldn't help it. Every time he saw her, it was brand new.

He took a deep breath and exited the driver's seat. "Catch," he said, throwing her the key.

Karalee looked completely confused as she caught it. "Why are you giving me the key to your SUV?"

"It's belongs to you," he said, opening the driver's door fully for her.

She stopped dead in her tracks and her eyes widened. "What are you talking about?"

"It's your company car."

Her mouth dropped open and she continued to stare at him.

"Your truck should be fixed and ready for pickup later today, but this is your car for work."

She shook her head and thanked him.

"Well, what are you waiting on? Let's go," he said, unable to stifle his chuckle from the shocked expression still on her face. "I need my assistant to drive me around today."

She looked even more shocked as she moved to the SUV. "So we're not going to the office?"

"No." He smiled and stuffed his hands into his slacks. "I have business meetings outside of the office all day. You don't mind spending the day with me and driving me around, do you?" he asked.

"Not at all," she said coolly before moving inside, but he could see her heart beating out of her neck. Her hands even trembled slightly as she started the SUV.

A wide smile covered his face as he closed the door and moved inside the SUV. The radio was on and the announcer was reading the daily horoscope about his sign, the ram.

Usually he didn't heed to such nonsense, but today it was on point. "Love is in the air," the announcer said. "The lover you've been dreaming about is near." He looked at Karalee whose magnetic eyes just happened to be on his. He had a strange feeling that for once the horoscope prediction was true.

7

Marcus sipped his drink inside Liberty Bar & Grill. The popular restaurant stayed packed and served the best wings in town. The only pitfall was the noise. Thankfully he and Karalee sat in a secluded spot where the sound from the crowd was blocked out.

They were laughing over a college story Marcus had just finished telling her. Still chuckling, he turned his attention to his Rolex and realized Alejandro was late. A sinking feeling made his stomach turn.

"So what kind of meeting are you having today?" Karalee asked, distracting him.

"I'm finalizing paperwork to open Tucker Insurance in Madrid."

"Spain?" Karalee's eyes twinkled.

"Yep." He looked at his watch again. "In fact, the property agent, Basilio, flew in from Spain. He should be here any minute now. I just hope Alejandro gets here before he does."

"Who's Alejandro? "Karalee asked, speaking the name beautifully.

"Our company's Interpreter and translator. Basilio only speaks Spanish, so Alejandro is translating for me today."

The ringing of his cell broke his attention. Noticing it was Alejandro, Marcus answered immediately. "You're late. Where are you?" He leaned back in his seat and spoke into the phone. His stomach churned as he listened to Alejandro's excuse. When the conversation was done, he snapped the cell closed and dragged his hands down his face.

"Is everything okay?" Karalee asked, looking concerned.

"No; Alejandro was just called away to a family emergency. He's not going to be able to make it. He's sending another Interpreter, but he won't be available until this afternoon." Marcus shook his head. "I've been working tirelessly for the past two years for this day. I'm not about to wait until later to finalize things." He was about to call Emily when he noticed Mr. Basilio heading his way. "Here he is now." He stood from the table completely stressed. "I don't know how I'm going to explain any of this to him."

"Don't worry about it," Karalee said, standing quickly from her seat next to him.

"What do you mean?" Marcus asked, entirely confused as she extended her hand to Mr. Basilio.

"Hola!" Karalee said, ignoring him. She shook the balding man's hand. "Como estas?"

"Grande," Mr. Basilio said, smiling as he returned the handshake.

Marcus could not close his mouth as Karalee began speaking rapid Spanish to him.

"What did you just say?" Marcus asked when they stopped speaking.

"That I'm going to be your Interpreter for today," Karalee answered.

"You didn't tell me you could speak Spanish," he said, still shocked as they all sat.

Karalee cut her eyes at him. "Spanish and French," she said humbly before chatting away with Mr. Basilio.

Marcus shook his head in amazement. Karalee was incredible! She continued to surprise him. Plus, hearing her speak Spanish was sexy as hell. He felt his nature trying to spring to life, but he reminded himself how imperative it was to finalize the paperwork.

For the next two hours, Karalee proficiently interpreted back and forth between him and Mr. Basilio. They signed the remaining paperwork and scheduled a date for Marcus to visit Spain to look at the new headquarters. When the meeting was over, Mr. Basilio stood from the table. He shook Karalee's hand, and then said something to him before gathering his files and moving away.

"What did he say?" Marcus asked, anxiously.

"He said: welcome to Madrid," Karalee laughed.

Marcus turned fully to Karalee. She was about to leave to head to the restroom, but he blocked her in.

"I'm buying you lunch" he said, staring down into her sexy eyes.

"Again?" Karalee asked, looking surprised.

He slid in closer. "Yes; believe me; you deserve much more than lunch."

Karalee wanted to ask Marcus what he met when he'd said she deserved much more than lunch. Did he see her as special? She was sure he had encountered some amazing women in his time being he was well-traveled and successful. How did she make an impression on him in such a short time? Still, the words made her feel a sensation she'd never felt in the pit of her belly.

As they ate she took in the beautiful restaurant. She'd never been to a place like this before. The restaurant was huge. There were three levels of seating and each had to be about 20 feet high. A big open area, with a rock climbing wall that looked like two side by side mountain peaks crowned the center. From their table they had a perfect view of people racing to the top of the mountain peak. Whoever made it to the top first sounded a bell and won a tee shirt. She couldn't help but to chuckle at the competitive people.

Marcus pushed his half eaten plate away, distracting her. He leaned back in his seat and stared at her a few seconds before speaking. "I'm confused about something."

"And what's that?" she asked, pausing her fork over her seasoned baked potato.

"You are a very smart woman," he complemented. "With your education, you should be higher than a personal assistant."

Karalee's heart dropped and she looked away. "I entered the work force later than most," she answered.

"How come?" he probed, circling the straw in his tea.

"My mother was ill and I had to take care of her." She looked back at him, noticing the curiosity intensifying in his gaze. She knew he wanted to find out more, but she couldn't tell him about her past-not if she wanted to keep this job. Swiftly, she changed the subject. "That rock climbing wall is incredible. I've never seen one that big before, and I've never seen one in a restaurant."

"You want to try and climb it."

"Try?" She placed her fork down. "I used to climb rock walls all the time when I was in college."

"You don't strike me as the type of woman to climb rock walls."

She cocked a brow. "And what's that supposed to mean?"

"No offense, but I surmised you'd like doing softer things."

"Ha!" She slammed the cloth napkin to the table. "You're so wrong. When I was little I was a complete tomboy, and I still am."

"Really?" Marcus smirked. He took a sip from his drink.

"I can show it to you better than I can tell you," Karalee gawked at him.

"Is that a challenge?"

"Sure is," Karalee shot back.

Marcus leaned in on the table. "If there's one thing you must learn about me: it's the fact that I love a challenge," he said, keeping his eyes trained on her.

Karalee almost shivered. She had a strange feeling the words were directed to her. Pulling herself somewhat together, she leaned on the table and matched his intense stare. "I love challenges too," she shot back. "I bet I can get to the top of that wall before you."

He narrowed his sexy eyes. "And what will happen if I win?"

"You won't."

"But if I do, you will have to cook dinner for me Friday night at my place."

"Are you serious?"

"Yeah; I haven't had a real home cooked meal since my chief died last year. Can you cook?"

"You'll never find out." Karalee said, with fire in her eyes. "Let's go."

They moved downstairs and the staff gave them properly fitted climbing shoes.

Marcus smirked at her as the staff helped her into a harness.

"I can't wait to eat your cooking," he said, licking his lips.

Karalee had to look away. The site of him licking his juicy lips were enough to mess her head up completely. Instead, she focused on the wall and mentally noted potential handholds and footholds. She placed one foot in a foothold at the lower level.

When Marcus shouted the number three, she grabbed a handhold on the rock wall above her head and took off.

You can do this, she encouraged herself. The last thing you want is to cook dinner for that fine man at his place. Only God knows what will happen if you're locked in a tight spot with that face and body. You will surely come out of your panties!

Minutes later, she cut her eyes to check Marcus's progress. Her mouth dropped when she saw him way up ahead of her. Was he Spiderman? His long legs moved swiftly up the wall with no signs of slowing down.

She cursed. Already she could feel her arms burning and fatigue kicking in and she was only midway. Fighting past the exhaustion, she took quick steps. She could pass him. I will pass him, she psyched herself up. Remaining focused, she left him in the dust.

Arrogantly, she looked down and smiled before waving to him and mouthing the word goodbye. In her haste, she missed the next step. She dropped and was swinging in the air. She heard a buzzer and looked up. Marcus had made it. He'd won and he was cheering and laughing like a fool.

Less than a minute later, she was safely on the ground. Marcus smiled at her as he finished putting back on his shoes. He thanked the staff for the T-shirt and declined on the pitcher of beer they also said he'd won. He moved to her and placed a hand on her shoulder.

"Oh, by the way," he said, fighting not to smile. "I love homemade mac and cheese.

Karalee tried to huff as he moved away, but she could only smile.

8

Friday evening, Marcus took off his suit jacket and grinned before he grabbed the groceries from the back of the SUV.

Karalee rolled her eyes heavenward. "Are you seriously going to wear that tee shirt all day?" she asked, taking a bag from him. "It's bad enough you wore it to work."

"Hey, I won fair and square," he said, closing the trunk, "So deal with it."

Karalee shook her head as they stepped toward his triplex home. All week she hadn't been able to focus on anything but this moment and being alone with him. Still, what scared her most was cooking for him.

"This place is big," Karalee blurted out. She stepped beside him and looked over the large property lined with trees which gave it ultra seclusion. She could only stare in awe at the beautiful triplex. "Do you live by yourself?"

"No; my cousin Carlos just moved in with me," Marcus said, placing his two grocery bags down and pulling out his house key. "But other than that it's just me. I'm a complete loner."

Karalee chuckled.

"What's so funny?"

"I don't know. You just don't seem like the type of man who'd be a loner."

"Believe me, when you're in my position, its best to surround yourself with as few people as possible. My circle is very small," he said, opening his front door.

Karalee moved inside and tried to close her mouth, but she couldn't. The place was incredible and spacious. She was sure Summer's entire home could fit inside. Every room perfectly captured the light whether it was the floor to ceiling formal living room or great room. She took in the marble fireplace, impressive spiral staircase, porcelain floors and the beautiful view of a lake outback. The furniture was trendy and the wall paintings were unlike any she'd ever seen. She didn't realize she was just standing there and staring until Marcus cleared his throat.

"Did you just hear that?" he asked, moving beside her.

"Hear what?" she asked, turning to look into his handsome face.

"My stomach just growled. Why don't I show you the kitchen so you can get those pots to bumping."

She shook her head as he took the bag from her and placed it in the kitchen. Quickly, he gave her a tour of the beautiful home. Afterwards, he guided her back to the kitchen and showed her how to work the humongous stove.

"It's all yours." He winked an eye at her. "I'm going to get out of this tee shirt."

"Thank you," she said, clapping."I am sick of seeing it."

"Just have the mac and cheese bumping by the time I come back." He ordered playfully, before moving away.

Karalee gathered the supplies and got busy. A few seconds later, she heard the shower water running. A shiver crossed her spine when she thought about him being butt naked with water cascading down his incredible body. For once she wanted to let her guard down and jump into the shower with him. But no matter how badly her body told her to do it, she couldn't. She wasn't that type of woman. She considered herself decent. Still he was bringing the ho out of her more and more every day.

She shook her head and busied herself preparing the dish.

Less than then fifteen minutes later, she had the mac and cheese in the oven. She studied the dials on the humongous stove and tried to remember how he'd told her to operate them, but she'd forgotten.

She saw the bake light and turned it on. Afterwards, she washed the residue from her hands and leaned on the counter.

Once again, she began daydreaming about how Marcus looked naked. A dreamy smile covered her face.

The next thing she knew she smelled something burning. Turning, she noticed she had the oven on broiler instead of bake. She tried to turn it off, but with so many buttons it was impossible. She looked inside the oven. The mac and cheese was browning quickly. She had to get Marcus.

She moved to the bathroom door. She was sure the water was still running. She knocked several times but there was no answer. He obviously didn't hear her.

Karalee tried to think. Should she go in and tell him? Or let the macaroni and cheese burn? What if she burned down the entire home? In a matter of minutes the delicious tray would probably be in flames.

Swallowing the lump in her throat, she moved inside. Steam clouded the bathroom along with his manly scent. Her entire body ached and trembled and the pearl between her thighs hardened like a rock.

"Marcus!" she shouted weakly. She covered her eyes with her hand and inched closer to the shower and called for him again.

Suddenly, she felt a presence behind her. Dropping her hand and turning, her eyes landed directly on Marcus Tucker's magnificent chest. He was shirtless and only wore slacks. She could only drool.

"Found what you're looking for?" he asked, smiling sexily before moving closer to her.

"Good God almighty," she muttered. She tried to say something else, but she was speechless. She lustfully took in everything from his bulky deltoids to the tattoo of a woman etched on the right side of his abdomen. The man was so cut and ripped he looked like he was about to pose for a fitness magazine.

Inching backwards, she braced herself for what was to come. From the look in his eyes, he was about to take her into his arms and kiss the living daylights out of her. She knew what would come next: her skirt would be hiked up and her panties would be yanked aside. Then he'd placed her weak legs across his shoulders and have his way with her.

Weak, she back into the wall and closed her eyes, waiting to feel the touch of his juicy lips. But to her surprise- nothing. Opening her eyes, she watched as he reached for the towel behind her.

He wiped the remaining water from his massive chest. She felt like a fool. The man wasn't thinking about sexing her. He was trying to finish dressing.

"You know, it's very rude to sneak up on a man in a shower," he said, placing the towel back on the rack and grabbing his shirt.

"I-I wasn't sneaking up on you." she stuttered, barely able to stop staring as he covered his chest with the shirt.

"Oh yeah," he smiled. "Then why are you in here?"

"I'm trying to keep your house from burning down," she snapped. "I can't turn the boiler off."

Instantly, the smile vanished from his face. He darted from the bathroom, leaving her alone. Karalee leaned on the wall to gather her bearings. Every nerve in her body was on fire. She shook as his body continued flashing in her mind.

***

Why didn't you just kiss her, Marcus chastised himself as he took the dish from the oven and quickly placed it on the kitchen counter. He wanted Karalee so badly he felt like he was about to go out of his mind. It had been close to a year since he'd had sex with a woman. Having her so close to him in the bathroom had aroused his nature to the point where he'd contemplated taking her against the wall, and sexing her until their legs gave out.

He leaned on the counter and tried to get his breathing and nature under control. Karalee was more than a sexual fantasy. He loved her mind. She constantly challenged him and kept him thinking. He wanted to make her his and keep her around. He couldn't believe she'd managed to cut through his layers of concrete and expose his heart in such a short time. It frightened and excited him at the same time.

Focusing back on the dish, he noticed it had not burned. In fact, it was perfectly crusty and browned. Unable to control himself, he grabbed a spoon and delved in. Suddenly the taste of flour and too much salt had him racing to the trashcan. He spit the soupy mix from his mouth and moved to the sink. He took a big gulp of water, praying the awful taste would disappear. After drinking the entire glass, his mouth returned to somewhat normal. "Yuck!" he said, shaking his head. "What the heck is that?"

He turned around and Karalee was near the kitchen door.

Rage and hurt clouded her eyes."That's what I was trying to tell you!" she shouted angrily. "I can't cook!" She grabbed her purse and rushed to the door.

Shocked by her outburst, he chased after her. He grabbed her by the arm, halting her. "Wait a second," he said, turning her to him. "It wasn't that bad."

Karalee managed a non humorous laugh. "You shouldn't lie; I can see your nose growing, Pinocchio."

Marcus chuckled. "Okay, it tasted bad-really, bad," he admitted.

Karalee looked even more dejected.

"But just because you mess up in one area doesn't mean your entire life is ruined. So what you can't cook. You're a very smart woman. You can learn; can't you?"

Her breathing slowed some. "I guess," she said, sounding a little more upbeat.

"Then let me teach you."

She put a hand on her hip and cocked a brow. "Wait a minute? You mean to tell me you can cook?"

"Yeah, my chief taught me."

"Then why would you ask me to if you already knew how?"

He decided it was time to cut the bull and be honest. "I wanted to spend more time with you," he confessed.

Shock covered her face, followed by a brief silence. "And why would you want to do that?" she finally asked.

He slid in closer, aligning his face and lips evenly above hers. "I like having you around," he continued speaking honestly. "I mean, I never know what I'm going to get from you. One minute you're cursing me out and the next you're speaking Spanish."

They both shared a laughed.

She shook her head and uncertainly clouded her gaze again. She looked away before she spoke. "Marcus, I'm just an average woman."

He lifted her face to his. "Believe me, there is nothing average about you." He traced the outline of her heart-shaped chin."You're very special."

Instantly flames began burning in her eyes, turning him steel hard right away. Swallowing his fears, he lowered his mouth to hers. She did not resist and what followed was a kiss so hot and steamy, it left them both panting.

Unexpectedly, he felt the pressure of her hand on his chest and she broke the kiss.

"Marcus… I can't." She tried to turn away, but he grabbed her wrist, pulling her back to him.

"Am I the only one feeling this chemistry between us," he asked, easing in until no space was left between them.

A groan erupted from her throat, and her eyes fired up even more.

"I thought not," he said, pressing his lips to hers and continuing the delicious kiss. His body took on a mind of its own then. Before he realized what he was doing he was backing her toward the oversized sectional while he hiked up her skirt. He followed her down onto the couch and pinned her underneath him. Quickly, he eased between her thighs. The sensations of her femininity pounding against his steel hard arousal drove him insane. He broke the kiss and trailed his lips across hers. "Damn, I want you," he moaned. "Tell me you want me too."

"Marcus-"

"It's a yes or no question," he said, kissing her neck.

Her eyes sparkled with lust, and she groaned the words he wanted to hear. Unable to control his desire, he began a slow grind against her center that had them both going insane. Tired of the wicked teasing, he sat up and lifted her directly onto him. He was sure she could feel his throbbing hard on. It felt like it was about to burst from his jeans.

Grabbing her by her buttocks, he stood and lifted her up high above him. The lusty kiss continued as he headed for the stairs. Just as he was about to take the first step upwards, the front door opened.

"Hey cuz," Carlos said. He stopped dead in his tracks and stared in shock as he eased Karalee down onto the floor.

Marcus wanted to curse. "I wasn't expecting you back so early." He muttered instead. "I thought you had football practice."

"Thank goodness it was cancelled," Carlos said, moving to him and staring at Karalee as she quickly righted her appearance. "Hey ma." He shook her hand.

"Her name is Karalee," Marcus corrected.

Carlos ignored him and continued staring. "Cuz, you gotta hook me up. I hope she got a sister just as fine her," he said, slowly roaming his eyes over every inch of her."

"Please excuse us," Marcus grabbed Carlos by the arm and pulled him away. He couldn't believe his idiot cousin had come in and messed up everything. "What are you doing?" he asked, through clenched teeth. "She's my assistant."

"Looks like more than an assistant to me." Carlos chuckled.

Marcus squeezed his eyes closed at a lost for a comeback.

Carlos began laughing and clapping his hands. "Oh shoot; you like her, don't you?"

"We'll talk later," Marcus said before he shoved Carlos into his room. He closed the door while he was still speaking.

He took a deep breath and headed back to the living room. "Please excuse my cousin," he said, strolling into the living room." He was shocked to find Karalee was gone. He rushed to the window just in time to see her SUV exiting the parking lot.

***

Marcus Tucker's sensual kiss left Karalee trembling most of the night. She could not sleep. She was not going to be rested for work tomorrow. She had to meet Marcus at the gym at nine. It was almost five a.m. All she could think about was the kiss they'd shared and the way he'd been working up against her. My God that man can move his hips, she thought, trembling again. A slight smile made its way across her face as she thought about the thickness and length she'd felt pressed against her. Judging from the feel of it he had a very lengthy…

The sound of the television distracted her. Snow White had sat on the remote, accidently turning it on. She grabbed the cat and placed her next to her.

Deciding to keep the television on, she turned to a paid advertisement. The dull advertisements always put her to sleep in the past. About twenty minutes later, she finally dozed off.

Marcus Tucker appeared in her dreams. Things started just where it had left off. He took her upstairs and placed her on his bed. She felt the weight of his body as he spread out on top of her. He felt amazing!

She wanted to kiss every inch of his magnificent body, and she wasn't about to wake up until she did.

She moaned as his skilled tongue began licking her ears and lips. Slowly, her hands traced and kissed every ripple of his eight pack stomach. Noticing the bulging muscle below, she undid his jeans. When she saw the pulsating length, she flipped him over, ready to giddy up.

"Karalee!"

What was Summer doing in her perfect dream?

Karalee blocked out her voice. It was just getting to the good part.

"Karalee!" Summer called out to her again.

She wanted to tell her to shut up and go away. She was disturbing her from the best dream ever. But it was too late. She felt her body floating away from Marcus. She grabbed his hand, hoping she could remain in dreamland, but she came back to the real world.

"Will you go away?" Karalee mumbled, trying to drift back off to sleep and continue with the dream.

"Okay, I'll go. But you're gonna be late for work," Summer warned. "And why is that cat licking you all in the mouth and on the ears like that?"

Karalee's eyes opened wide. Snow White was lying on her chest, purring and licking her lips.

"Eww!" She sat up and tossed Snow White off of her.

"What time is it?" Karalee asked in a sleepy tone.

"You have a half hour to make it to work."

Karalee stood from the bed and rushed to the dresser to gather her clothes.

Underneath her clothes, she found a roll of money. "I have something for you," she told Summer. She moved to her and gave her the money she'd gotten from pawning her engagement ring. She'd also added over half of her paycheck to the roll.

"How'd you get this?" Summer asked, staring at her wide eyed.

"Don't worry about it." Karalee smiled; glad that she could help out a little.

"Did Marcus give you this?" Summer continued to probe.

"No. Why would you think that?"

"He got that company car for you."

"Listen; don't worry about how I got the cash, okay? Just go pay your bills," Karalee ordered.

"Thank you, sis," Summer said, bouncing happily to the door.

She stopped and turned around. "Oh, don't forget the 4th of July is this Monday."

"I know; no work. What are you going to do to celebrate?"

Summer smiled. "Well, I was hoping you and I could go camping on Lee's Lake."

"The one grandma used to take us to every 4th when we were little."

"Yeah; I already got everything set up. It's just gonna be you and me."

"I can't wait," Karalee smiled. She headed into the bathroom. She was about to undress when she realized she was out of soap.

She headed to the closet upstairs to get some.

On the way, she passed Summer's bedroom. The door was halfway opened. She noticed Summer giving Spider a roll of money. Spider began counting it.

"That should cover everything," Summer said, sitting on his lap.

"Thank you, baby." Spider said, kissing her. "As soon as I get this child support caught up, I'll be able to help you out some around here."

Summer put her finger over his mouth to shush him. "I got your back, baby," she said before wrapping her arms around his neck and kissing him.

For a few seconds, Karalee could only stare in complete disgust and confusion. She couldn't believe Summer had used her money to help Spider with his child support. What kind of man did that? And what kind of sister took money from her struggling sister to take care of a bum? She'd not only pawned her engagement ring, but had given her over half of her first paycheck.

She was so angry she wanted to barge into her room and go off, but instead she grabbed the soap and went back to the basement. She would deal with Summer later. For now she had to worry about Marcus Tucker and how she would get through the day without kissing him again.

9

"Second Chance Gym & fitness," Karalee mumbled as she pulled up to the entrance of the address Marcus had given her. She grabbed her gym bag and exited the car. The young men outside eyed her like she was the first female they'd ever seen. Maybe the shorts and printed tee she wore was a little too revealing, but Marcus had told her to dress comfortable and to bring a change of clothing.

"I'm looking for Marcus Tucker," she said, strapping her bag across her shoulder.

One of the guys opened the door and pointed out where she needed to go. Moving inside, Karalee noticed an empty waiting area and an office. She heard Marcus's deep voice telling someone to punch him.

Butterflies played in the pit of her tummy as she remembered all that had happened yesterday. She was excited about seeing him today. Curious, she hurried around the corner and into a big and spacious gym. What she saw made her knees buckle and her heart stall in her chest.

Marcus Tucker was half naked inside the boxing ring and sparring with a young man. He only wore boxing shorts and sneakers.

Weakly, she sat in the first chair to prevent from collapsing to the floor. Lustfully, her eyes took in everything on his built body. For a few minutes, she stared openly, forgetting she was in the gym.

Unexpectedly, his eyes connected to hers. A devilish grin covered his striking face. The room seemed to flip right along with her heart.

He told the young man he was sparring with to take a break. He stepped from the ring and moved to her. She took a deep breath and tried to steady her wobbly legs as she stood to greet him.

"Why did you run off like that yesterday?" he asked, toweling his body dry.

"Your cousin sort of..." she searched for the right words.

"Ruined everything," Marcus finished for her.

She nodded.

"Well, he's spending the rest of the weekend with my sister. I was hoping you could come over after we're done here."

"That sounds good," Karalee agreed. She forced her eyes to look over the spacious gym and not at his perfects pecs or the V-shape disappearing into his shorts.

"So what do you think?" Marcus asked. He spread his hands out and looked over the gym.

"This place is amazing," she complimented. "You didn't tell me you were a boxer."

"I'm not," he said, continuing to towel his body dry. "I teach boxing as a way to release stress and anger. These young men learn how to control their temper and plus, being here keeps them off the streets."

Karalee couldn't hide her shock. "So you volunteer here?" she probed.

"This is my gym," he revealed."

Karalee nodded, unable to hide her awe. "I sure wished I had a place like this to come to when I was a teen."

"That's exactly why I opened it. I needed a place like this when I was a teen too. If it wasn't for my gym teacher introducing me to boxing as a way to release stress, I don't know where I would have ended up. Let me show you around," he said, moving before her.

Karalee bit her lower lip and followed. After seeing the front part of him she didn't think it could get any better, but the back end of him was just as satisfying.

When they were done with the tour, he led her to an office and showed her the basic work she would do which included keeping track of attendance and supplying the young men with fresh towels and water. A group of young guys interrupted and Marcus was off to the ring again.

Like an addict, Karalee followed. She spent the next few hours watching Marcus in action inside the ring and handing out bottles of water and towels. The way

Marcus encouraged and disciplined the teens won her completely over. He was a selfless man. He could have been anywhere on the weekend, but he was dedicating his time to helping young boys become men. There was no way she would ever look at him the same.

Laughing distracted her. She noticed a group of young ladies had entered and were near the ring cheering Marcus on. One in particular caught her attention. She was the oldest of the crew, maybe in her late twenties. Long Brazilian weave hung down her back. The way she was meagerly dressed, and showing off her bubble butt as she eyed Marcus, made Karalee experience a sudden wave of jealousy.

Shocked by her emotions, Karalee dragged in a deep breath. There was no way in hell she'd let another man make her feel emotional in any sort of way.

Smiling, Marcus exited the ring and called Karalee over to him. He was about to speak with her when bubble butt stepped in between them.

"I'm assuming you lost my number," the woman said with an island accent. "I thought for sure you'd call me."

Karalee turned and left before she could hear the remainder of the conversation. She was afraid she wouldn't be able to stomach it. She entered the office and dropped into the office chair, busying herself with work. What had she expected? A man as fine as Marcus Tucker had plenty of women vying for his attention and throwing themselves at him. What did she care anyway? She snatched papers from the printer and began banging instead of typing on the keyboard.

She lowered her eyes to the desk. She couldn't lie to herself any longer. She wanted him! Not only was she strongly attracted to him, but she liked the person he was. He had completely impressed her and now she was infatuated with him.

There was a light tap on the door. Marcus stood in view.

"Hey; you got time to come practice with me."

"Why?" She asked, unable to hide her attitude. She stood from the seat with a folder and headed for the file cabinet. "Don't you have bubble butt

to practice with you?"

"Bubble butt?" he asked, looking confused.

"Yeah," she huffed. She mean mugged bubble butt and the other women through the glass as they all cleared out of the gym.

Marcus smiled when he followed her gaze and realized who she was glaring at. He blocked her from opening the file cabinet. "Do I detect some type of jealousy?"

She forced herself to laugh. "Never."

"Really?" He asked with disbelief etched on his face. He grabbed her wrist and pressed two fingers against it.

"What are you doing?" she asked, annoyed.

"Feeling your pulse, and judging from the way its beating, I'd have to say you're not being truthful."

Karalee snatched her hand away and placed the file in the cabinet, trying hard to steady her heart.

He smiled and moved in until no space was left between them. "I must admit, I like this."

"Like what?"

"You being angry. It shows that you are just as infatuated with me as I am with you."

The words made Karalee's heart skip several beats. She snatched up the boxing gloves and faced him. "I'll show you how much I'm infatuated with you when I tear your butt up in that ring," she said, trying to change the topic.

"Hey, we're not competing," he corrected her as they moved outside of the office. He locked the gym doors before they moved to the ring. "Were boxing as a way to release stress and to discharge anger."

She hopped inside and leaned on the ropes for support. "Well, I'm not angry and I don't have any stress that needs to be released."

"Really?" Marcus smirked, walking the short distance to her. "Well, I remember a certain woman who cursed me out the first day we met. What was that really about?" he asked.

Embarrassed by her past behavior, she lowered her head.

"You don't have to tell me anything, just use my body as a punching bag. Come on; hit me."

Karalee raised her gloves, but she couldn't punch him. She'd never physically fought anyone in her life.

"Take your gloves off," he ordered.

Karalee did as she was told. He pulled off his gloved too.

"Now, close your eyes."

"Are you serious?"

"As high cholesterol," he answered.

His response made Karalee chuckle. She took a deep breath and did as he instructed. He moved in closer, towering over her. He grabbed her hands and took them into his.

"I want you to think about something- anything that made you so mad you wanted to just kick somebody's ass."

Karalee cracked one eye open and looked up into his striking face. "Are you some sort of therapist?"

"Just do it." he ordered.

Karalee shook her head and closed her eyes, but she was unable to let her feelings go.

He slid in closer and told her to open her eyes. He used his hand to lift her chin. "Trust me on this, okay?"

As Karalee gazed into his eyes she experience the same strange feeling of safety that she'd felt when he'd taken her home on his motorcycle. She nodded.

"Now, close your eyes," he said gently. "I want you to think about that person who made you angry. Remember what they did to you and how they made you feel."

The past came back to Karalee in flashes. She saw the empty apartment, and the blood dripping down her legs. She heard the doctor telling her she'd miscarried. She remembered being released from the hospital in pain only to return to an empty and lonely apartment to heal on her own. She saw Chris in the newspaper hugged up with his agent.

"Now open your eyes," he ordered. "Let's go! I want you to release all of your anger here."

Karalee snapped from her memories. When her eyes adjusted, she no longer saw Marcus, but Chris standing before her. Emotions she'd held at bay came bubbling to the surface. She felt tears burning her eyes as she put her boxing gloves back on and focused on his chest.

Before she realized it, she'd landed a punch to his abdomen. She landed another punch, and then another, all the while cursing in between.

"You coward!" she shouted, punching him again.

 "How could you leave me like that?"

Punch!

"After all those years I wasted with you!

Punch!

"I loved and trusted you."

Punch!

"I thought you loved me too."

A few seconds later, she'd backed Marcus into the corner, continuing to land blow after blow. She hadn't even realized she'd trapped him in the corner until he grabbed her by the arms to stop her. He turned her around, pinning her against the ropes.

"Karalee!" He shouted twice.

She blinked from her trance. Dazed, she looked up. Chris was gone and Marcus remained.

"You have one hell of a punch," Marcus said out of breath.

He smiled, but all of Karalee's emotions came to the surface like an erupting volcano. She started crying uncontrollably as everything came gushing out. Her legs buckled, causing her to collapse.

Marcus caught her in his arms and eased her down to the floor on top of his lap.

"It's okay," he said, rubbing her back as she continued to cry. "Don't hold it in. Let it all out."

She didn't know how long she cried. All she knew was she felt so much sadness, anger and confusion that she could not stop. As she cried, a heavy weight began to slowly lift from her chest. She felt relieved.

Once the tears finally stopped flowing, embarrassment set in. This was the first time she'd ever let her emotions out in front of anyone. Now her cement shell was broken and she felt exposed. She tried to speak-to apologize, but Marcus shushed her.

"Don't you dare apologize for hurting." He pulled her closer and held her tightly while he consoled her. You're only human and stuff hurts. It's okay to feel that pain and release it. Housing pain and anger inside your body is dangerous. That's why I teach this sport."

As he continued consoling her, Karalee experienced the same feeling of safely again. She rested her head against his chest. When the sniffling stopped and her chest no longer heaved, he planted a kiss to her forehead and then to her nose. She looked up and noticed the same lusty look she'd seen in his eyes yesterday. But only this time it was mixed with affection. When his lips came crashing down on hers, she didn't attempt to stop him.

Her mind went blank and without hesitation, she let his tongue plunge into her mouth. They kissed slowly and deeply, while his hands gently zigzagged down her back.

Something strange happened as the kiss intensified. Karalee connected with him. She realized he understood her pain and that it was okay to share her feeling with him. Never would she feel uncomfortable talking to him again, nor would she hold back. She was safe. When the kiss ended, she was breathless. He rested his forehead against hers and steadied his gaze on her.

"You want to get out of here?" He asked, stroking her chin.

"Where to?" She managed a wobbly smile.

"How would you like to learn how to really cook mac and cheese?" He asked, before helping her from the floor.

***

I'm already catching feeling, Marcus thought completely surprised and confused by his emotions. He slid his chair closer to Karalee. They were outside on his terrace that overlooked a private lake, and music was playing in the background.

As he spooned another helping of mac and cheese onto her plate he tried to figure out why he felt such a strong connection to her. They hadn't even had sex, but he was enthralled by her personality. She was an enigma to him. He just couldn't figure her out. One minute she was strong and outspoken, the next minute she was weak and vulnerable like a baby. One thing was for sure: she would not get rid of him easily. He had every intention of snatching her off the market and making her his.

"I wish I could cook like this," Karalee said, bringing him from his reviver.

"I'll keep practicing with you." He lowered his fork over the seasoned baked chicken. "Remember, you can cook anything as long as you follow the recipe. In time you will be comfortable enough to try this on your own."

"I don't think I'll ever be able to cook like this, but it sure is fun learning. Thanks for teaching me."

"My pleasure. I have a lot more recipes to teach you, so that means we'll be together a lot."

Karalee smiled and held her glass out.

He poured her another round of sweet punch. "So, are you going to tell me about Chris?"

Karalee wiped her mouth with her napkin." I thought I told you everything about him at the gym."

"The only thing I know is that he hurt you."

"Badly," Karalee said, looking away.

"Go on," he encouraged her, glad that the wall she'd had up was down.

Her eyes became distant. "The day he left me was the worst day of my life," she said, pushing her plate aside. "Not only did I lose him, but I lost our baby."

Marcus listened in horror as she shared everything from how he'd emptied their apartment, to how she'd been forced to move in with her sister. Suddenly, everything about why she refused his help made sense. He felt bad for her and angry at Chris. His past relationship flashed before his eyes but he couldn't share it now. At the moment he had to comfort her

"He's a coward," Marcus muttered.

"I feel the same way. I mean, at first I didn't. For a long time after he left I was sad," she continued, looking dejected. "I thought that I'd done something wrong or that something was wrong with me."

He slid his chair closer, rubbing her back. "Oh Karalee. Trust me. There is nothing wrong with you. You're amazing. You're smart and beautiful in every way."

"I know that now; it's just that when a man dumps you in the way that I was, it does something to your self esteem."

"Believe me. What he did is no reflection of you; it's a reflection of him. Chances are he will do the same thing to any woman he gets with because the issues are within him."

One of his favorite slow jams from back in the day was playing in the background.

"You feel like dancing?" he asked, wanting to lift her spirits.

She nodded and he held out his hand, helping her up. He guided her away from the table to another part of the deck. Holding her tightly against him, they moved in synch with each other as the artist crooned words of love, trust and happiness.

God, she felt good and she smelled even better! He wanted to take her upstairs, lay her on his bed and take his time pleasing her. But he pushed the thought away. He had to let her know that he had no purpose of playing games with her. Still dancing, he lifted her face to his. "I hope you know I meant what I said yesterday and today. You're very special, Karalee."

She shook her head. "I thought you were just saying things in the heat of the moment."

He brushed his finger across her lips. "I don't just toss out compliments. Anyone who knows me will tell you that."

"What about bubble butt?"

"I'm not interested in that woman at the gym," he said seriously. "I only want you."

Her eyes widened in surprise, and he could see her heart beating out of her neck. Bending his head, he took her lips and they kissed, slowly and passionately. When the kiss ended he was breathless.

"Do you think you can spend the rest of the weekend with me?"He asked, sounding and feeling desperate.

"I wish I could, but I already made plans with my sister."

He tried to hide his disappointment. "We'll, if things change, let's do something together."

"Like what?"

"I don't know; you plan something. Surprise me like you always do."

She laughed, and he pulled her back tightly into his arms. When his member tried to grow, he fought it off. There would be time for that later. For now he held her closely, with plans to dance the night away.

***

Karalee was feeling overwhelmed and happy at the same time as she pulled out her house key. She was still in shock over all the events that had transpired today. What Marcus had done at the gym for her was incredible, and the romantic dinner was amazing. She couldn't stop humming as she placed the key in the lock. The love song she and Marcus had danced to was still playing in her head. She couldn't believe she was humming like a fool in love, but the more she was around Marcus, the more she could feel her control slipping away. She was falling hard for him, and there was nothing she could do to stop it.

She closed the opened door and moved inside. A ball flew by, barely missing her face. It landed on a picture on the wall. The picture crashed to the floor.

Her eyes landed on a little boy no older than four or five with big brown eyes and a snotty nose.

"Who are you?" Karalee asked.

The little boy stuck his tongue out and ran, hiding behind the sofa.

"Thomas!" Summer yelled from the other room. "What did you break this time?" She thundered into the living room and was about to say something when she noticed Karalee.

She told Thomas to go clean his nose and to get ready for dinner. She sat on the chair, massaging her temple. "Look, I'm not gonna be able to go camping with you tomorrow. You're gonna have to find somebody else to go with you or go by yourself. I have to babysit."

"Whose child is that?" Karalee asked, taking off her heels.

"Spider's," Summer said, popping an aspirin into her mouth and taking a sip of bottled water.

"What?" Karalee shouted.

"Will you calm down," Summer said through clench teeth. "You're gonna wake the baby."

"You mean to tell me he has two children?" Karalee asked, walking to the chair in front of her and dropping in it.

"He has five and they are all here for the weekend."

Karalee was flabbergasted. "Wait a minute," she said, holding up her hand when she could finally gather her thoughts to speak. "Let me get this straight. You're not only paying Spider's child support, but you're babysitting his five children too?"

"Who told you I was paying his child support?" Summer asked, looking drained as she popped yet another aspirin into her mouth.

"I saw you give him the money I gave you this morning."

Summer took a sip of water and sat forward, looking pissed. "What I do with money you give me for rent is none of your business."

"You're right, but this is wrong on so many levels, Summer. You shouldn't be taking care of a grown ass man and his kids. You're sick. Did you forget you have Lupus?"

"Look Karalee, he's having a hard time right now."

"He's having a hard time alright," Karalee muttered. "Since I've been here I haven't seen him lift a finger to do anything. He isn't even trying to find a job."

"Hey, you have no room to talk."

"And what do you mean by that?"

"All I'm saying is you're not perfect. How can you judge my man when you couldn't judge the man you were with? Did you know he was gonna leave you and run off with another woman like that?"

The words sliced Karalee's heart. Feeling numb, she stood from the couch.

Summer stood too. "Karalee…I'm sorry. I didn't mean that."

Karalee held up her hand and left the room.

She moved to the basement and sat on the bed. She could hear the children running through the house and a baby wailing. She had to get away for a few days and blow off some steam. She checked to see if the weather would be nice for the weekend. After she confirmed it, she grabbed her bags and packed. She was going camping. She pulled out her cell phone. She knew just the person to take with her.

10

"Ouch!" Marcus hit his arm, trying to kill whatever insect had just stung him. Confused, he looked around the forested environment. When Karalee had invited him to spend the remainder of the weekend with her, he'd been elated. During the two and a half hour drive, he had surmised she was taking him to a nice, cozy place where he could be along with her, and hopefully sweep her off of her feet. Never in a million years would he have thought they would be in the woods, in the middle of nowhere.

"What is this place?" Marcus asked as Karalee opened the back of the SUV and pulled out a cooler.

"Lee's lake," Karalee said as she continued sorting through things.

"I'm confused," Marcus admitted. "Where are the hotels?"

Karalee laughed. "There are none."

"So where are we gonna sleep?" he asked, hitting yet another insect that had stung him.

"In a tent. We're camping."

"Camping?" his voice squeaked.

Karalee stopped rummaging through the things in the back of the SUV and stared at him. "Don't tell me you're scared." She started clucking like a chicken.

"I'm not scared of anything," he said, laughing now that he sounded like her, and she sounded like him.

"Well; what are you waiting on? Grab a backpack and the cooler."

Marcus placed the backpack on his back and lifted the heavy cooler. He followed Karalee down a dirt trail for what felt like an hour, but was really no longer then twenty minutes. By the time they made it to a clearing, he was sweating and tired. He sat on the cooler and soon his butt was hurting.

He studied Karalee who looked right at home as she got busy pulling out all sorts of things.

He liked Karalee- a lot, but he didn't know if he would be able to survive two days out in the woods. He'd never done anything like this and was used to being in civilization.

"When I told you to surprise me you went all out, didn't you?" He laughed as he looked at the woods surrounding them.

She moved to him and sprayed insect spray on his arms. "Hey; I promise you're really going to enjoy this."

He was about to tell her he seriously doubted that.

The only good thing would be spending time with her. But before he could say anything, she flashed him a smile that made him forget everything. Suddenly the insect bites no longer bothered him, or the fact that he was out in the middle of nowhere.

He couldn't help but to smile back as he stood to help her.

She taught him how to set up the tent. They gathered rocks so she could build a campfire later. Then they took two air mattresses to a store located less than a mile away from their camping site to fill them with air. By the time they returned to their spot, it was a little after noon. Marcus was starving.

"Can you please tell me how we're going to eat for two days being you can't cook?"

She shook her head and ordered him to sit down in a chair she'd unfolded.

Soon she returned with a platter of drinks, sandwiches and other snacks.

She gave him hand sanitizer and sat the patter before him on a fold out table.

"I may not be able to cook, but I can make one hell of a sandwich," she teased as she sat on the chair next to him.

"Yes you can," Marcus agreed as he took another big bite from his chicken salad sandwich.

As they ate, it suddenly dawned on Marcus how peaceful and nice the environment really was. Having money had exposed him to a lot life had to offer, but he'd never been exposed to nature. It was priceless. The air was fresh and free of smog. He could hear birds chirping, there was greenery all around and beautiful mountains in the distance. The both of them laughed when a squirrel came up and grabbed some bread Marcus had dropped.

He looked at Karalee who was lost in her own observation of the scenery. He wanted her more than he'd wanted any other woman before.

"Hey, let's go for a walk," Karalee said, snapping him from his thoughts.

Swiftly, she discarded their trash and grabbed her backpack.

Soon, they were walking along a beautiful trail with the sun blaring in the distance. Marcus was in complete awe. Never before had he seen so many birds and exotic looking plants in his life. Karalee stopped and picked berries from a tree.

"Taste," she said, offering him one.

"I'm still stuffed from lunch; I'll pass." He turned his nose up.

"Come on," she urged, popping one into her mouth. "They are delicious."

He took one look into her eyes and knew he could not tell her no. "Alright," he finally conceded. She smiled and placed one in his mouth.

"This is good," he chirped as he enjoyed the sweetest berry he'd ever ate. "What kind of berries are these?"

"Blackberries and stop eating them," Karalee said, taking the one he was about to pop into his mouth. "I just wanted you to taste. Let me wash them first."

He helped her filled a canister with berries and soon they were moving again.

He grabbed her hand and kissed it before taking it into his. They walked hand in hand, enjoying nature.

A few minutes later, they came to a beautiful rest stop with a bench that had gorgeous flowers and statures all around it.

They sat to drink bottled water and to rest.

"So your grandmother used to bring you here?" he asked, breaking the silence.

A gorgeous smile covered her face as she turned to him. "Yeah, every 4th of July. She loved this place being my grandfather proposed to her right here."

"Where we're sitting at now?" Marcus asked.

"Yep; over sixty years ago." She stood and moved to a tree.

He followed. There was a heart and two names etched in the center. "Granddad did this," she said, tracing the names and the heart.

Marcus smiled as he traced the outline after her.

"I never got to meet him," she continued, "but grandma always bragged about what an amazing man he was. After he died, she couldn't look at another man. She never remarried, because to her, no man could touch him."

Marcus leaned against the tree and pulled her into his arms.

"Maybe we can repeat the past?"

"What are you talking about?" she asked, smiling up at him."

"I want you to say the same thing about me sixty years from now."

Karalee chuckled and brushed him off. He realized she had no idea he was serious.

"We're living in a me, myself and I generation," she said, moving back to the bench. "That kind of love doesn't exist anymore."

"Oh yes it does." He sat next to her. "Love doesn't fail people, Karalee. People fail love."

"Exactly, I don't want to put myself out there again. I mean I put my heart on the line before and looked what happened."

He slid in close. "I was in love before too." It was his turn to share and Karalee gave her undivided attention. "I was seeing several women and not looking to settle down, and then I met this beautiful woman that made me forget about all the others. We dated for a short while, and I gave up everything for her. We got engaged and were planning a wedding. A week before the ceremony, she disappeared, taking a big chunk of my money with her. I tried to find her, and that's when I discovered she was not who she'd said she was. Everything from her name to her place of business was bogus."

He heard Karalee gasp and then a knowing look reflected in her eyes.

"After that, I was suspicious of all women. I thought they were only interested in sweet talking me and getting their hands on my wealth. But then I met you, and you curse me out and told me no twice."

They both laughed. He turned serious again. "You're realness is refreshing. You're different, Karalee. Very special; and now I realize that just because someone failed with loving me the way I deserved to be loved in the past, doesn't mean I should give up on love in the present. Neither should you."

"That makes sense," she said after a few seconds of silence.

"What; really?" he laughed. "This is the first time you didn't challenge me."

She hit him playfully before he pulled her face to his.

A serious kiss took place that made him forget everything. He loved kissing her. Already he could feel blood racing through his body and swelling a place that didn't need to be engorged at the moment.

She pulled back and stroked his square jaw. "It's going to be dark soon." She stood and grabbed his hand. "We'd better head back."

Finding the willpower he didn't know he had, he stood and followed her.

By the time they returned to the camp, the sun was slipping behind the mountains. The weather had cooled, and Marcus helped Karalee build a campfire. They sat near the blaze and roasted hotdogs. She taught him how to make her grandmother's S'mores.

Afterwards they lay on a blanket, talked and ate the berries they'd picked while watching the stars twinkling overhead. Time passed too quickly and Marcus noticed Karalee had drifted off to sleep.

He studied her as she slept. With the crackling fire burning nearby, he got a perfect view. She had almond shaped eyes, a full nose, sexy heart shaped lips and flawless skin. His gaze slid over her body. He felt his arousal. Her figure was perfect. He could see her hardened nipples through her tee shirt, and he knew her breast were full and perky. She had a flat stomach and her legs were long and toned. However, her butt was the enticing part that had him going bananas. It was round and perfect. He remembered how good it had felt squeezing it when she'd been at his place. He wanted to feel it again. His arousal stood fully.

He placed a fingertip on her lips and traced the outline of her mouth. Damn he wanted her! The need to have her was so overpowering he was afraid he wouldn't be able to hold off much longer. Kissing her gently, he woke her up. Karalee yarned and smiled up at him.

"So I guess you're ready to turn in for the night?" he asked.

"Yeah, I'm beat," she said, not opposing as he leaned in and kissed her again. She pulled away and stood. "We'll sleep next to each other."

His pulse thudded from her words. When she moved off the blanket, he silently cheered. They were going to be alone in a tent with no one to hear or disturb them. Quickly, he moved to put out the campfire.

When he turned around, Karalee was setting up another tent. "What are you doing?" he asked, moving to her.

"Getting ready for bed."

"But I thought you said we were sleeping next to each other?"

"We are; but in different tents."

"So you're not going to be afraid all alone?" he asked, helping her set up.

"Please," she said. "I've been camping since I was a little itty bitty thing. Nothing out here scares me."

"Okay, but don't disturb me tonight when you hear something growling in the woods."

"In your dreams," she said. She disappeared in her camp and returned with clothes. She headed to campground shower that was a few feet away.

A half hour later, she returned. He didn't expect her to look so exotic in a pajama short set, but she did.

When he leaned in to kiss her goodnight, he had to restrain himself from dragging her into the tent with him. She smelled good-like the flowers he's smelled in the woods earlier, and her warm body made the blood race through his veins and engorge his male hood. He pulled away, not wanting her to notice. "I really had a good time today."

"Tomorrow will be even better," she promised.

He watched her disappear into her tent. He grabbed a change of clothes and headed to the shower. The cold water cascading down his heated body did the trick of calming him. He changed into a long sleeve, button down shirt and shorts and returned to his tent.

He entered and turned on the glow lamp. He rested on the air mattress, but he couldn't find a comfortable spot. After tossing and turning for what felt like forever, he finally settled down. As he listened to the bird and insect sounds, all he could reflect on was his life and how it had to include Karalee.

11

Karalee had planned for everything for the camping trip- except the rain. The weather report had said it would be sunny for the rest of the weekend. She had checked it several times. But now it was raining cats and dogs. It was cold too. Even though she had a blanket wrapped tightly around her, she was shivering.

A loud clap of thunder sounded again. The ground seemed to tremble it was so loud. She put her head under the cover. She'd never admitted it to anyone, but she'd always been afraid of thunderstorms. Being out in a tent in the middle of a storm petrified her. She tried to breathe normally as the rain beat down on the tent.

Powering on her cell, she noticed it was a little after one. She considered going to Marcus and staying in his tent until the storm passed. But she quickly dismissed that thought. Not only would he think she was scared, but she knew her legs would not stay closed if she was alone with him. She had strong feelings for him. Most of the day she'd been fighting off her need for him. It was almost getting impossible to resist.

Boom! Boom! Pow!

Karalee sat straight up on the air mattress when she heard the thunder.

"Forget this," she said, grabbing her sleeping bag. She placed it over her head and exited the tent. Quickly, she darted out into the pouring rain and moved to Marcus's tent.

"Marcus!" she called for him twice before he unzipped the opening to his tent.

For a moment, she forgot what to say when she saw his shirt wide opened. His chest was everything she needed at the moment to help her forget about the storm.

Wide. Muscular. Kissable.

Shaking her head, she took his hand as he helped her inside. She looked at him, noticing sleep was in his eyes.

"How can you sleep through a thunderstorm?" she asked, trembling as she sat on the fold out chair.

He cracked a smile. "Don't tell me you're scared."

"When I told you I wasn't afraid of anything, I lied." She sneezed. "I hate thunderstorms."

He removed the wet blanket from around her. "Why don't you sleep on my bed until the storm passes?"

She moved to his air mattress and cuddled up under the blanket on his bed. Instantly, she began to shiver when she smelled the intoxicating scent he'd left behind. "Aren't you cold?" She asked, trying to ignore the heat that was starting to thaw out her womanhood.

He sat on the folded chair. "A little; but I'll be okay. You need to stay warm."

He sneezed three times in a row.

Karalee felt bad as she rested her head on his pillow. Here he was catching a cold because of her. She opened up the blanket and hit the spot on the bed next to her. "There's room for the both of us," she said before she had a chance to think.

With no hesitation, he eased beside her. The warmth of his flesh made her whole body start shivering with need for him.

Loud thunder sounded in the distance. Karalee jumped and trembled. Quickly, Marcus took her into his arms. "It's okay," he whispered, kissing her forehead. She could feel the heat of his sweet breath on her face. She didn't have the courage to look into his eyes.

He lifted her chin, forcing her to meet his gaze. The fire burning in his orbs instantly thawed out her frozen flesh. He traced the outlined of her lips with his finger before staring at her again.

"I don't think it was a good idea for me to get in this bed with you," he said, sounding more like he was panting instead of breathing.

Karalee knew the reason why he'd said such a thing. She could feel his manhood poking into her stomach. Still, she swallowed her fears and asked him why.

"Because I'm not going to be able to resist you," he said, sliding in closer. He eased his hand through her hair, bringing her face closer to his.

Karalee swallowed the lump in her throat. She wanted him too! Now was not the time to punk out. She brushed her lips against his, and looked boldly into his eyes. "Who said I wanted you to resist?"

Before she could blink, his mouth came crashing down on top of hers. The kiss was wild and wet. Soon their moans drowned out the sound of the rain.

Karalee felt his heart out pounding hers. She wanted to see him naked. Swiftly, she ripped off his shirt.

Marcus broke the heated kiss. "I can't be the only one shirtless," he teased, undoing her pajama top and tossing it aside.

Immediately they started tearing off each other's clothes and undergarments, kissing in between. They did not stop until the other was gloriously nude.

Marcus pulled the cover off of them and lay on his side.

Karalee gasped when she took in his entirety. She'd never seen him completely nude. Seeing him naked made the pearl between her thighs harder than a rock. His body was amazing! Every part of him was cut and toned. She didn't know whether to stare, worship or touch him. She looked up, noticing his gaze was trained on hers.

"Why did you stop?" she asked, trembling from the intensity of his stare.

"I want to see all of you," he said as his eyes swooped up and down over her slowly and lustfully.

"Do you like what you see?" she asked, feeling her confidence dip.

"No, I don't like it." He moved in until no space was left. "I love it."

Karalee could not hide her sharp breath intake as he captured her lips, kissing her again.

"You're beautiful…so damn beautiful," he said, easing back on top. He kissed her for a while before his tongue left her mouth. Hot and wet, it trailed down her neck before moving to her breasts. From one nipple to the other he suckled, squeezed and teased until she felt like she was about to go out of her mind.

His free hand played over the rest of her aching body. It moved down her quivering tummy and rested on the curly hairs shielding her hotness. When two of his fingers slipped between her labia, and teased her hardened pearl, she almost cried out from the intense pleasure. A second later, his face lowered and replaced his fingers. She climaxed instantly. The aftershocks were so strong it left her convulsing and mumbling his name.

He grabbed her legs and gently pulled her down to him. "I love the way my name sounds coming from your lips." He planted a light kiss on her mouth. "I want to hear my name again when I'm inside of you."

She put her hand on his chest, halting him. "I don't have protection," she moaned.

"I do," he said, securing his book bag that was near them.

"You always carry condoms around?" she asked, staring at the pack he'd pulled out.

"No, but I had a feeling this weekend would be special. I couldn't leave home without them." He kissed her and turned his attention back to the condom. As he sheathed his manhood, Karalee could only drool at the lengthy, hard throbbing gift he'd been blessed with. She could hardly wait to feel it moving inside of her.

He eased between her wet, trembling thighs. She lifted her legs higher and wrapped them tightly around his back. She could barely breathe as he slid inch after glorious inch inside of her. After she adjusted to his hardness, he began to move in a rhythm that should have been a sin. The pleasure caused her to squirm against the crumpled sheets.

She bit her lip as she touched and caressed every rippled of his stomach and back. When her hands reach his butt, she grabbed it and pushed him in deeper.

Exotic words spilled from the both of their lips.

Wanting to see him in the midst of pleasure, she opened her eyes. What she saw made her gasp. Electricity more powerful than the flashing lighting outside blazed in his orbs.

"Don't hold back," he whispered, kissing her in between his thrust. "Give me all of you. I want all of you."

"Whatever you want." She tugged his earlobe between her teeth and began to move with him. Soon, the only storm was the one they were creating together. She felt thunder and lightning moving through her body as he hit areas that had never been touched before. Areas that connected to her heart and soul. Areas that connected her to a part of him.

He brought her to a screaming climax that left her gasping for air. Seconds later, his eyes clouded. His large hands gripped her hips. His thrusts became faster-impatient. He moved up and down, moaning in between. He did a final thrust. His eyes disappeared into his head as shudder after shudder rocked his body. When he rested on her chest, her arms circled him and pulled him in tighter.

Marcus's head was clearer than it had ever been in his life. He saw his relationship with Karalee clearly. She was the woman he would spend his life with. If he had it his way, she would walk down the wedding aisle with him and be the mother of his kids.

A half hour had slipped by. Marcus was still too tired and satisfied to move out of the spot he and Karalee were cuddled up in. Karalee had given him a sexual experience he'd never had with any other woman. He'd not only been pleasured out of his mind, but he'd linked with her beyond sex. She was the one. He'd felt it before, but now he knew without a shadow of a doubt that she was made for him and he for her. He wasn't about to let her get away.

For now, he was on a mission to earn her trust. Trust that had been shattered by people who had used and taken advantage of her good heart. He would show her he was not like Chris. He was going to love her and help her get her life back together physically and emotionally.

He kissed Karalee's neck. She smiled up at him.

"I feel like I'm dreaming," she said. "I keep thinking I'm going to wake up and find out this is not real."

His heart sunk from her words. "It's real; No one will ever hurt you again."

"Ever?" she looked up at him with shock in her eyes.

"That's right. I'm not going anywhere." She smiled and rested her head on his chest.

A loud clap of thunder sounded in the distance and she tensed. "It's okay; the storm will be over soon." He comforted her.

"I hope so," she said, gently rubbing his arm.

"Why are you afraid of thunderstorms?" he asked, playing in her hair.

Karalee looked up at him and her eyes lost the sparkle he loved. "When I little, my dad left my mom. After he left, my mom would always leave my sister and me home alone. Sometimes for days. She was on anything that got her high. She did everything from huffing paint to popping pills. Most of time when she disappeared, we didn't have food and the lights and water was always disconnected.

Marcus noticed the pain in her eyes intensifying as she continued.

"One day mom said she was going to her friend's house. I was angry. We didn't have food. I knew she wouldn't come back for a few days, so when she left, I followed her. When she realized I was with her, she made me sit outside on the carport at her friend's house. She said she didn't trust the men inside and told me not to go anywhere until she came back to get me. A bad storm came while I was waiting."

Tears fell from her eyes and Marcus wiped them away.

"I sat in that storm crying for hours before someone called the police.

My grandmother got full custody of me and my sister after that. She made my childhood amazing."

Marcus smiled when he saw the light return to her eyes.

"We didn't have much," Karalee continued. "But grandma was determined I was going to college. She worked extra jobs and paid for me to learn Spanish and French. I was in every school spelling bee too. I wasn't allowed in the kitchen, so I never learned to cook. She wanted me to keep my head in the books. If it wasn't for her, I don't know where I would have ended up."

Marcus massaged her shoulder. He felt his heart beating in sorry for her. He understood her pain. Her trip down memory lane brought up memories of his childhood. Memories that was too painful to think about, so he focused on her instead. "Is your grandmother still alive?"

"No, she died when I was seventeen. I reached out to mom after grandma passed. By that time she was living on the streets and still getting high. I moved her into my grandmother's house and put her in rehab. I had just gotten a scholarship to attend college, but I put off going to help her. Every time, she would stay in rehab for a few weeks and then ditch it."

Marcus slid in closer and stroked her cheek. "You know, you're the most unselfish person I've ever met."

"I was just doing what any daughter would have done," she said, shrugging off the compliment. "I'm no angel."

"Close enough. I don't know many young people who would have put off college like that."

"I just wanted her to get clean." Pain was in her tone. "I would have done anything to make that happen."

He lifted her face to his. "You can't fight other people's demons, Karalee. She'll accept your help when she's ready."

"I know, but I still worry about her."

"That's only natural. Trust me; your mother will return when she's tired."

Karalee nodded.

Marcus propped up on his elbow and looked down at her. "Until then, I want to make you happy."

She smiled up at him." I want to make you happy too."

His heart rate increased. "I can think of one way you can make me happy now." He moved in closer.

"And what's that?"

He climbed back on top of her. "I think I'm going to need help easing something down."

"Oh, that shouldn't be a problem," she said, laughing as he turned her over to straddle him.

The muscles in Karalee's leg tightened in pain. Groaning, she sat up straight out of her sleep. She massaged the aching muscle until the pain ebbed. Just as the ache disappeared, her other leg began cramping. She groaned and moved her attention to the hurt muscles. As she rubbed the ache away, a smile crept up on her face. She pondered the events from last night. Marcus had kept her legs hiked up above his shoulders half the night. She was sure that was the reason why she was sore now. Smiling like a fool, she looked over and noticed he was gone.

The opening of the tent was cracked and she got a glimpse of the sunlight. The storm had passed and it appeared the day was going to be beautiful. The weather reminded her of her life. She'd been through hell. Now it appeared the sun was breaking through the clouds. She prayed it stayed this way forever. She didn't think she could handle heartbreak again. Just as she was about to get up and inspect to see where Marcus had gone, he came through the tent carrying two cups of steaming coffee.

"Good morning sleepy head," he said, placing the drinks on the fold out tray before sitting down and kissing her.

"How did you sleep?" she asked, wrapping her arms around his waist.

"Like a baby with you next to me." He lay down and pulled her next to him.

"Well, I'm glad you're well rested," She purred, kissing his neck. "You will need your strength today."

"I know," he said, easing his hands down her back." She felt his hand cupping her bottom.

"Oh, no." She stood from the bed in her undergarments and grabbed her clothes. "Our activities are taking place outside of the tent, Mr. Tucker."

"What do you have planned?" He folded his arms behind his head and stared at her.

"Something really nice." Karalee said, stretching. She noticed his eyes almost popped from his head when she leaned over to retrieve the remainder of her clothes.

"You're trying to tempt me, aren't you?"

"I am not," she blushed as she slipped on her pajama top.

"We'll it's too late; you already have." He stood and chased her around the tent. When he caught her, he pulled her back onto the air mattress with him.

"What are you doing?" she asked, fighting playfully against him.

"I want to make love to you." he said, placing his hands on either side of her face.

"But what about my plans?" she protested.

"We can do whatever you've planned later," he answered, pulling the covers over the both of them.

***

"Can you please explain how we are going to cook fish?" Marcus asked Karalee a few hours later. They'd been sitting near the river for an hour with their fishing poles inside the water. Even though he was enjoying the breeze, the smell of the water, and especially Karalee, he was growing impatient.

"Don't worry," Karalee answered. "The store that sold us the bait will clean and cook whatever we catch."

"If we catch anything," he added, leaning in to kiss her nose.

"You have to be patient," Karalee advised. "Besides, I like sitting out here and talking to you."

"I like talking to you too," Marcus smiled.

"So are you going to tell me whose picture that is you have tattooed on your abdomen?"

Marcus felt his heart drop. "My mother," he answered, keeping his gaze trained on the river. "Who'd you think it was?"

"An ex girlfriend." She admitted. "You're mother looks so young. How old is she?"

"She would have been sixty if she were alive."

"What happened?" Karalee asked, moving in closer. He saw sorrow and concern in her eyes.

"Heart attack," he muttered. "She passed away when I was fourteen."

Karalee rubbed his back and told him she was sorry. He felt his heart rate increasing. He didn't want to think about his mother now. Whenever he did, he was forced to think about what had happened after her death. Too painful. Too many bad memories. He wanted to enjoy the trip and Karalee. He was feeling too good to travel down memory lane.

His fishing pole began jerking. He was happy for the distraction.

"Oh my God; you have one!" Karalee shouted. She moved in front of him and grabbed his pole, helping him reel the fish in.

After struggling some, they pulled out a beautiful, big fish from the water. Marcus laughed, feeling like a kid as they both lost their balance and landed on their butts in the sand.

He looked on proudly at the fish flipping and flopping on the edge of the pole. He helped Karalee up from the sand. They high fived each other. This is the best trip ever!" he shouted as he dropped the fish into the bucket.

"I told you you'd catch one, didn't I?" Karalee stared at the fish.

"That's a pretty big one," Marcus said. "We can share it for dinner."

"Are you sure that's going to be enough for the both of us?"Karalee asked. "Your appetite has increased lately."

"I wonder why?" he asked, pulling her to him. A wet kiss took place that made him heated from head to toe. "You know, you may be right," he added once the kiss ended. "One fish probably isn't going to be enough." He wrapped his arm around her waist. "I'm going to make sure you and I are well fed. We are going to need our strength tonight."

They both laughed as he grabbed her hand and guided her back to the river.

12

That night, after their delicious fish dinner, Karalee was shocked when Marcus took her for a ride away from the campsite into town.

Now they sat, wrapped together on a paddleboat experiencing fireworks from the lake.

"This is amazing!" Karalee said, looking on in awe at the fireboats in the river shooting patriotic streams of fireworks high into the air. "How'd you find out about this?"

"The guy at the store told me this morning when I went to get coffee."

He kissed her forehead. "This is the best getaway I've ever been on," Marcus admitted. "I'm having a great time."

"So am I," Karalee said, resting her head against his chest. She felt his heart thudding. There was no denying that she was in love with Marcus. He was a wonderful man, and she felt lucky. Still fear crept in. Things like this only happened in dreams. It seemed too good to be true. After Chris, she had thought she'd be alone. Now her entire life had changed. She was happy and scared at the same time.

"I have a surprise for you when we get back into town," Marcus said, bringing her back to the present.

"What is it?" she asked, pulling her eyes away from the fireworks and looking up at him.

"I'm not telling you." He wrapped his arms tightly around her waist. "Just know that I am going to help you get back on your feet."

Karalee squeezed her eyes closed. The last thing she wanted was for a man to help her get back on her feet. Chris had done the same thing when she'd been released from prison. He'd supported her and her mother and then left her high and dry.

"Marcus, I appreciate everything you've done for me," she said, stroking his arm, "but I don't want anything given to me. I want to earn and get everything on my own."

He was about to say something when a clap of thunder sounded in the distance.

Chills raced down Karalee's spine. Alarmed, she sat up. "I think we'd better go," she said, happy their boat was close to shore.

"Chill out," he said, pulling her back to him. "It's nothing." He rubbed her goose bumped skin.

Karalee tried to settle down, but then she felt light rain on her arms and face. She knew a storm was coming. She was not about to take a chance and be caught in it.

"Marcus…please." She felt her entire body trembling. "I want to leave." Marcus stared at her curiously for a few seconds before he began rowing back to the shore. Once there, he began collecting the things they'd brought from the vendors.

A flash of lighting brightened the heavens. "Leave it!" Karalee said impatiently. She hurried off, shoving her way through the viewers gathered on the shore.

She cursed. She'd never trust another weather report again.

In no time she found the parking lot. She tried to remember which row the SUV was parked on. She heard a rumble of thunder again."Where is the freaking car," she mumbled. The parking lot seemed to be spinning and she felt sick. She felt a hand on her back. Startled, she jerked around.

It was Marcus.

"Why'd you leave like that? It's just a passing storm, baby." He pointed to the heavens and she noticed the clouds were quickly fleeting.

"We'll, I'm not taking a chance. I want to leave."

She tried to pull away, but he stopped her. She looked at him like he'd lost a screw in his brain. "What are you doing?"

"Making you face your fears. It's time you stop running. You're not that little girl sitting alone in the rain waiting on your mother anymore, Karalee. So please tell me what are you are afraid of? Is it really the storm or is it me?"

Her heart began pounding faster from the question. "Marcus, this is not the place or time." she said.

"Sure it is." He grabbed her by the shoulders and looked into her eyes." I'm not your mother or Chris. I wouldn't do what Chris did to you. I'll protect you. I'm here."

Her emotions came bubbling out. "Are you?" she asked, wiping her nose.

"What do you mean by that?"

"People leave, Marcus. They always do. After they get what they want or they grow tired of the person, or a storm of life appears, they walk away, leaving you alone to pick up the pieces. At the end of the day the only one I have is me."

Hurt clouded his gaze. "You think I'd hurt you... leave?"

"Eventually," she said. "I mean, a man of your caliber...what's going to keep you here?"

"Love," he answered.

She gasped and looked at him. "Why would you say that?"

"Because I mean it. I feel it. You felt it too. What we shared last night...today was more than sex. We connected." He took her face in his hands and for a moment, she forgot it was raining. "I'm in love with you, Karalee."

She shook her head and looked into his eyes. They were filled with affection. "I love you too," she finally admitted.

His eyes darkened with emotion. "Then don't let you fears ruin this-us." He pulled her into his arms.

Karalee felt her heart surrendering as she rested her head against his chest.

When he pulled away, he extended his hand. "Will you trust me? Come back to boat?"

Karalee took a deep breath and looked into the sky. He was right. It had been a passing storm. The rain had stopped and the moon was peeping out. She looked at his outstretched hand. She took a deep breath and placed her hand into his, deciding to leave her fears in the past.

By the time Karalee parted ways with Marcus, she felt high. Nothing could bring her down. The trip had been better than she'd expected. She was in love with Marcus! She didn't know what was next. It was complicated and uncomplicated at the same time. She would just breathe and try not to let her demons from the past cloud her judgment. She entered Summer's house and headed for the basement. She was ready to unpack and relax before work tomorrow. Nearing Summer's room, she noticed the door was closed.

She thought she heard moans coming from inside. Her stomach clenched. She was sure Summer and Spider were doing what she and Marcus had spent most of the camping trip doing. But then she heard a crash and crying. She knocked on Summer's door. When there was no answer she opened the door. She noticed Summer's feet. She was on the floor, curled in fetal position.

"Summer!" She shouted, running to her. "What happened?"

Summer could only moan. "I don't feel good. My legs and arms are aching."

Karalee cursed and helped her to the bed. Trembling, she pulled out her cell phone.

"What are you doing?" Summer asked.

"Calling an ambulance."

"I don't need an ambulance." Summer tried to sit up, but whimpered in pain.

"Are you serious? You're sick as a dog."

"I'm fine," Summer protested. "I just overdid it this weekend."

Karalee moved to Summer's bathroom and grabbed her medicines that helped her arthritis and Lupus. "Where's Spider?" She asked after Summer took her pills.

She looked away. "At the basketball game with his friend."

"Are you serious? He has some nerve, leaving you here like this."

Karalee made sure Summer was as comfortable as possible. She moved to the kitchen and prepared a liquid broth for her. Then she called her doctor and set up an appointment for her to go for a checkup in the morning.

She fed Summer and gave her a sponge bath. Afterwards she got in the bed next to her. Summer didn't have on her lace front wig. Karalee saw just how much the lupus had caused her hair to thin and fall out. Her heart ached. She grabbed the comb and brush. Gently, she began fixing the little hair Summer had. "I want you to hear me out," Karalee said as she massaged conditioner into her scalp. "Spider is using you."

Summer looked away from her, but she noticed tears in her eyes.

"It's obviously he doesn't give a damn about you." Karalee shook her head. "He knows you have lupus and arthritis, and he left those kids with you all weekend."

Summer was about to protest, but Karalee cut her off. "You and mama are all I have left. I only want the best for you. I'm begging you, please let Spider go. He's dragging you down, sis. I will work and help you out with the bills. Just please, let him go."

Summer tried to speak, but Karalee shushed her again. She stood from the bed. "Don't say anything. Just think about it."

Summer nodded. A half hour later, Summer was snoring.

Karalee eased from the bed. She turned out the lights and left the room. Once in the hallway, she leaned against the door and looked to the ceiling. She prayed her sister would find the strength to move on.

Emily Tucker took an aspirin to stop the tension headache throbbing at the back of her skull. Sometimes she hated being the only girl born into the Tucker family. She wished she had a sister who she could share her worries with. Heading a colossal insurance firm was not easy and having five brothers and six half-brothers who constantly stressed her out didn't help. To make matters worse, her seventeen year old cousin, Carlos, had just moved to town to add to the pressure.

As she paced the living room of her 56,000 square foot mansion, she wondered why her father had placed the company into her hands when he'd fell ill. She also wondered why her mother had made her promise, on her deathbed, to steer her five brothers down the right path. Maybe it was because she was the only girl, or maybe she'd seen that she could handle it. That was far from the truth.

She loved her brothers more than life itself, but she didn't know how much more she could deal with their complicated lives. At least her brother Ford was happily married now to his lovely wife, Maya, and had added child number three to the family. That had eased the load some. But her other four brothers: Xavier, Marcus, Jayden, and Boris, were still not married. They always had some type of drama going down too that mostly involved women.

Her source of stress today was her oldest brother, Marcus. Everyone called him the protector of the family and he greatly deserved that title. He'd protected them during their childhood and was still very much the shield of the family. She could always count on him when trouble popped up in the family. That's why it bothered her now that she hadn't been able to get in contact with him for the last three days. That was not like him. He was always at his gym or a phone call away.

Where in the hell is he? She thought about calling the police, but what would she look like calling to report her grown brother as missing? He was a grown man free to go and do whatever he wanted. Still, she was worried sick. Out of all of her brothers, Marcus was the one who called her every day, and now that their cousin Carlos was staying with him, and spending the weekends with her, he checked in even more. It just wasn't like him to disappear.

She was afraid something had happened to him. Maybe one of the boys at his gym had done something. She'd always hated Marcus opened that gym and mingled with those young, troubled boys, But that was him, always trying to save people.

She heard a sound outside. When she saw Marcus's SUV pull into the driveway, she rushed to the door.

"Where in the hell were you?" Emily asked, breathing the biggest sigh of relief ever.

Marcus held up his hand. "Wait a minute; the last time I checked, I was an adult. Since when do I have to start answering to you?"

Emily shook her head."I was worried sick about you; that's all. I called your brothers, I went to your gym and house and you were nowhere to be found. I needed you. You have no idea what I've been through with that cousin of yours this weekend."

"What are you talking about?" Marcus moved to the kitchen and sat on the stool.

"You need to have a serious talk with that boy. He went to a party this weekend and when he returned, his entire left arm was tatted up."

"So what he got a tattoo? I have one."

"Yeah, but you got yours to cover up a childhood scar. His is plain unnecessary. I think he's trying to impress those girls. All he does is talk to them on that phone all day. I wanted to help him apply to colleges this weekend, but he was too busy. He went back to your place yesterday. I know you don't want to be too hard on him, but-"

"Don't worry, sis. I'll talk to him." Marcus cut in.

Emily breathed a sigh of relief. "So where were you this weekend?" she asked again, wanting to know.

Marcus bit his bottom lip and smiled.

The grin on his face confused her. He was also glowing. She'd hadn't seen him look like this in forever.

"Hello? Marcus Tucker; back to planet earth."

"I'm sorry. Did you say something?" Marcus asked, grabbing a bottle of water and breaking the seal.

Emily sat next to him and touched his forehead.

You don't have a fever, do you?

"Why would you think that?"

"Something's off about you." She folded her arms across her chest. "Spill it."

Marcus grinned again, and then he paused for a few seconds before turning to her. "I met someone special."

Feeling dizzy, Emily shook her head. "Wait a minute. Who is this woman?"

"My personal assistant."

Emily's blood pressure soared. "So you're dating an employee at the company?" She shook her head. "I must say that is a very poor decision."

"Why would you say that?"

"You won't look at this woman as a regular employee. Your judgment will be clouded. You won't know if you're basing your decisions on business or infatuation."

"Emily did you forget your best friend works for you?"

"Yeah, but that's different."

"How so?"

"We are two females. We stick strictly to business. However, men can't seem to keep their mind on business when a woman they want is involved. The small head replaces the thinking of the big one."

Marcus sighed. "Sis, just be happy that I'm in love."

"Love?" Emily's eyes almost came from the sockets. "When did all of this happen? I want to meet this woman."

"Hell no."

"Why not?"

"You're always digging up trouble."

"Really? Let's not forget, I investigated the last woman you were with. I told you something wasn't right about her. You didn't listen until a large amount of money came up missing from your account."

"You also told Ford that Maya was a bad idea," he said, referring to his brother and sister –in- law.

"Okay, so I messed up on that one time, but I'm right ninety-nine percent of the time."

Emily, look, just keep your mind on your own marriage. Focus on your man. Where is Stanley at anyway?"

"Right here," Stanley said, entering the kitchen and giving Emily a kiss. "Is my wife meddling in your business again?"

"You know it," Marcus said, grabbing his drink and heading for the exit.

"Hey!" Emily called out after him. She tried to follow him, but Stanley blocked her.

"Marcus is right. You need to worry about me. I'm feeling a little neglected."

"Really? During our sixteen year marriage have I ever dissatisfied you?"

"No, but between, the company, your brothers, sick father and now your cousin, I hardly get to see you."

"You know family and business are very important to me." Emily tried to move pass him, but he blocked her again.

"What about me?"

"You're very important too." She rubbed his trimmed beard. "You know how much I love you."

She tried to move pass him again to see if Marcus was still outside, but Stanley grabbed her hand into his.

"Why don't you come outside to the pool with me?"

"But-"

"No buts. Our sons won't be back from their school trip until tomorrow. We finally have the house to ourselves. Go put on a nice bathing suit and join me."

"I feel too old to put on a bathing suit."

He kissed her lips. "Nothing about you is old. You age like fine wine, darling."

Emily blushed. Her husband still caused her to get goose bumps after all these years. "Oh, alright. Let me change into my bathing suit."

The green one," Stanley said staring at her lustfully. "I love how you look in that one."

He guided her to the stairs and kissed her. By the time the kiss was over, Emily forgot all about Marcus and his new girlfriend.

13

Marcus pondered over the weekend after he left his sister's house. He took his sweet time driving home. He remembered the way Karalee had kissed and touched him. A shiver crossed his body. He wanted to do nothing but relax and think about Karalee when he arrived home, but he had a cousin- a very foolish cousin that needed some sense talked into him.

When he made it home, he saw cars parked in his driveway. He hurried inside. What he saw before him made his heart stop. Over ten young women, dressed in bathing suits were inside drinking and causing a ruckus.

Rage clouded his eyes. "Carlos!" he shouted, knowing he was the blame for this.

He felt like he was about to go out of his mind as he thundered into the main room and shut off the music. The place was in complete disarray and there were stains on some of his furniture. He thought he smelled smoke too.

"Carlos!" he shouted again, balling his fist. He was so angry he saw double? He went from room to room shouting for him and kicking people out at the same time.

He felt a soft hand on his arms. It was a young lady. She had a beer in her hand. "I don't feel so good. Where is the…"

Before she could finish the last word, she dropped the drink on the floor and barfed in an expensive decorative bowl he had on a stand.

Marcus helped the young woman to the bathroom. Afterwards, he continued his search for Carlos. He squeezed his eyes shut and inhaled before he moved outside onto the patio. His eyes almost popped from his head. Carlos was sitting inside his Jacuzzi with two young girls. One of them had a cigarette in their mouth.

Marcus wanted to snatch Carlos from the tub.

"Hey cuz." Carlos smiled as he exited the Jacuzzi. He even had the nerve to wear his robe. "I wasn't expecting you back today. I hope you don't mind. I brought some of my new friends from school over to chill out."

Marcus pulled him into an empty room inside the house and slammed the door.

"Are you on some type of medication I don't know about?" Marcus asked, his chest heaving.

The smile faded from Carlos's face."What's the problem?"

"What's the problem?" he almost shouted. He took a deep breath to quell his anger. "You have underage girls in my house drinking and smoking. Have you lost your rabbit sized mind? I don't have strangers in my home, and I certainly don't have wild parties here with under aged girls. It's going to take a month to get this place back in order." He heard a loud crash and both moved out of the room toward the sound.

He began shaking with rage. An expensive piece of artwork he'd purchased from China was shattered on the floor.

He wanted to snap Carlos' neck, but instead he swallowed his anger. "By the time I come back, I want everyone- including you gone. You can spend tonight at your aunts Emily's figuring out how you're going to pay for this mess," he said, before storming out.

Once outside, he hopped into his car and lowered his head. He really wanted to help his cousin and be a role model for him, but having a teenager in his house was not going to work out.

"Close your phone," Marcus ordered Carlos after he entered his bedroom the next morning. "You can call whoever that is back later." He looked around the junky space, completely disgusted. His cousin had turned his immaculate room into a pig's sty.

Carlos shook his head and closed his phone. He pressed the pause button on the game.

Marcus moved some clothes from the bed before sitting. "What you did yesterday was completely unacceptable. It will never happen again. Do you understand me?"

"Yeah; cuz and I'm sorry."

"Sorry isn't going to cut it. What would have happened if one of those girls got hurt? Or if the police came here and caught them drinking?"

"I didn't think about that."

"You didn't think at all, Carlos."

Carlos looked dejected. The last thing Marcus wanted was to be hard on the young man. When he'd been younger, he'd had it hard. He wanted to make Carlos's memories of his time with him great, but he knew he needed discipline. "So how are you going to pay for all of the damage?"

"I don't know. I don't got no job."

"You do now."

Carlos looked at him. "What kind of job? "

"Groundskeeper."

"Groundskeeper?"

"Yeah, at Tucker Insurance."

"You tripping."

"Hey; it's not even up for discussion." Marcus rose his voice an octave. "Every day after football practice, you are to report to my office and sign in. It will keep you out of trouble and help you learn how to be responsible."

Carlos let out a heavy sigh and nodded.

Marcus looked around the messy room again. "How can you stay in here?"

"What you mean?" he asked, pressing the play button on the game.

"This room is filthy."

Carlos shook his head and continued playing his game. "I'll clean it up."

"Thank you," Marcus let out sigh. "Anyway, what's this I've been hearing about you getting a tattoo?"

Carlos grinned and stopped the game. He took off his jacket and there was a big tattoo of a dragon on his left arm.

Marcus dragged his hands down his face before speaking. "Why did you do that?"

"The ladies." He curled his arm and his muscles bulged. "And why you tripping? You got a tattoo too."

Marcus shook his head. He knew everything Carlos was doing would equal up to trouble. "I didn't get this tattoo just for the heck of it." Marcus said, sitting on the floor beside him. "I was hurt when I was fourteen. My side was sliced opened. It left a nasty scar so I covered it with the tattoo of mom. He looked at Carlos's tattoo again and shook his head. "You need to slow down, man. They'll be lots of time for partying and girls later. For now you need to focus on getting onto college. Emily wants to help you apply."

"I don't think I want to go to college," Carlos admitted.

"Every Tucker goes to college."

"Yeah, but I'm the first Tucker who has a chance at being drafted into the NFL."

"You can't go from high school straight to the NFL, man. There is a three year after graduation rule in effect with the NFL office."

"I didn't know that." Carlos looked confused and disappointed.

"I know, and you're not going to know much of anything if you don't get a good education and keep your mind off these girls. What if football doesn't work out?"

"It will. I know it will," Carlos said with his eyes bright and foolish.

"Life doesn't always go as we plan," Marcus said, remembering how his entire life had been one big disappointment after another. "I just don't want you to put all of your eggs in one basket."

"I hear you, cuz."

"So are you going to let Emily help you apply for college?"

"I can do that," Carlos agreed.

"That's what I want to hear," Marcus said. He snatched up the second game controller and grabbed a pillow to put behind his back.

"What you doing?" Carlos asked.

"I 'm about to beat your butt at this game."

"Marcus what on earth are you doing?" Karalee asked. He'd called her in to work early. He'd met her in the parking lot and both rode up his private elevator together. Now, he was behind her with his hands covering her eyes as he guiding her to someplace unknown.

"Marcus, please tell me where we're going."

"Patience," he said, kissing her neck. They continued walking. She heard a door open and close.

"Okay, on the count of three. One, two, three…"

He dropped his hands.

It took a few seconds for Karalee's eyes to adjust. When they did, she noticed she was in a spacious office with a breathtaking view of the Atlanta skyline. She saw the biggest glass desk ever and a nice leather executive chair.

She moved deeper into the office. "What's going on? Why are we in here?"

"This is your office," he said, moving to her. He wrapped his arms around her waist.

Karalee felt woozy. She shook her head. "My office?"

"That's right. How does the title of Spanish translator and Interpreter for Tucker Insurance sound?"

"I'm not following you," Karalee said, barely breathing. Alejandro had to resign due to health issues with his wife. I knew you would be perfect for this position. You're work will include everything from converting written material, to orally translating and Interpreting at the company meetings. You'll also be my Spanish escort interpreter when we visit Spain this winter.

Weak, Karalee sat in the leather chair in front of the desk. "I'm going to Spain?"

"Yes, sweetie."

Karalee was so overwhelmed she could not speak. She wanted to cry. She had dreamed of something like this for a long time. Now it was happening.

Marcus kneeled beside the chair. "You deserve this Karalee. And I'm not giving you anything; you earned this spot fair and square. So what do you say?"

"I don't know what to say."

"Say you're ready to get to work." He stood and helped Karalee from the chair. He guided her to the big executive leather chair behind her desk. He sat down and pulled her onto his lap, kissing her.

Marcus hung up his office phone. He was happy that the work day was coming to a close. Today had been nonstop with back to back conference calls, and then meetings with key staff and his sister Emily. He stood from his desk and looked at his watch. His cousin Carlos had not reported to work today. He made a mental note to check him. He would be eighteen soon. He had to teach him to be responsible.

Marcus dragged his hand down his face. He was stressed. He wanted to end his day with Karalee. He'd invited her to his place, but she'd declined. Her sister was ill, and she was heading home to check on her. He was about to call to see if she could slip away later, but a knock on the door disturbed him.

"Come in."

Val moved inside with a troubled look on her face.

"Is there something I can help you with?"

"Yes. They sent a new woman in today who's replacing Karalee's.

"Yes, my new personal assistant." Marcus said, gathering files.

Val's eyes sparkled. "So Karalee didn't work out, huh?"

"She's here," Marcus said, snatching up his suit jacket and shaking it out. "She's in her new office."

Val looked like he'd just told her the world had come to an end. "New office?" she stuttered.

"Yes, she's been promoted to the company's Spanish Interpreter and translator."

Val's face reddened. "I'm confused."

"About what?" Marcus asked, grabbing his keys from the desk.

"How did she get a promotion in such a short time? If anything I should have gotten that position." He saw anger flashing in her eyes.

"No offense; but you can't do what she can."

"You mean sleep with you."

She mumbled it, but he'd heard it clear as day.

Marcus remained shocked for a few seconds before he spoke. "You're out of line, Val. Don't ever talk that way to me again. I respect you as an employee, and you will respect me as your employer."

Val took a deep breath and instantly looked apologetic. "You're right, I'm sorry. It will never happen again"

"Have a seat," Marcus instructed, moving back to his seat. He was completely confused. In the ten years she'd worked for him, she'd never said anything disrespectful. He had to get to the bottom of this now.

"I usually don't discuss my decisions with anyone," he said, sitting forward in chair and staring at her. "But in this case, I feel it is necessary. Karalee saved me at a meeting. Our Interpreter's wife was ill and he couldn't attend. I learned then that she was not only fluent in Spanish but could translate Spanish also. If it wasn't for her, I would have been delayed in finalizing the paperwork for our office in Madrid."

"I see," Val said.

Marcus leaned forward, braiding his hands on the desk. "I assumed you were happy with your current position, Val."

"I am, sir. Very happy." She smiled, but he could tell it was forced. "I appreciate this job and everything you've done to help me."

She apologized again before she stood and left the office. When she gone Marcus sat in his chair completely confused.

***

Marcus found Carlos outside of his private school, hugged up with some girl. He blew the horn. Carlos gave the girl a kiss before running to his SUV and jumping inside.

"You didn't report to work today." Marcus said time he slammed the door.

"My bad; it slipped my mind," Carlos answered, putting on his sunglasses.

"But that girl you were kissing didn't.'

"Don't trip; it won't happen again."

"I know it won't. I'm taking you to work now."

"Now?" Angrily, Carlos sat back.

"Yes; you have got to be more responsible. I'm telling you, my patience is paper thin. You are going to have to follow my rules or there will be repercussions.

"What you mean repercussions?" he asked, mean mugging him.

"The next time you don't come to work, everything will be taken from you; including you cell phone."

"How am I supposed to talk to my girlfriend?"

Marcus sighed. "Please tell me you're not dating that girl you were hugged up with."

"Her name is Kiki, and yeah, she's my girlfriend."

"You sure don't need a girlfriend."

"Why not?"

"You're too irresponsible and I'm telling you, that girl is trouble."

"Whatever cuz. She's straight."

Marcus shook his head and sped down the road. "I'm done with this conversation. This is my last time talking to you."

He glanced at his cousin who was busy texting on his phone. He had a strange feeling he hadn't heard a single word he'd said. He was headed for trouble. Marcus promised himself he would keep trouble from happening.

14

Karalee wanted to accept Marcus's offer for dinner, but Summer was still not feeling well. She wanted to talk to Summer and hear what the doctor had said. She checked on her right after she walked through the door later that night. She was in the bed sleeping peacefully. Spider was gone as usual. Karalee eased from the room. She moved into her basement room and flipped on the light.

Exhausted, she sat on her bed. She thought about the day and couldn't help but to smile. Marcus was something else! She didn't know how she'd pay him back, but she would. She thought about her new position. She loved being the company's Interpreter and translator. However, the day had been overwhelming and long. Her paycheck would look good next week though. She smiled, thinking about how much more money she would be making.

She was even looking into getting her own place. She was well on her way to being completely independent. She took off her shoes and was about to put them under the bed when she noticed Snow White was cowering underneath. "Come here, baby."

Snow White hissed and backed further under the bed. "What's the matter with you?" Karalee muttered. Usually Snow White met her at the door. She was about to drop to her knees to get Snow White when she heard movement behind her. She jerked around and Spider was at the back of her room, dressed in only his boxers.

She screamed and jumped on the bed. "What in the hell are you doing in here?" she asked, holding her chest.

Spider didn't answer. He continued to move toward her with burning rage in his gaze. "You like starting trouble, don't you?"

"You'd better get the hell out of here!" Karalee shouted, backing up on the bed.

Spider stopped at the foot of the bed. "And if I don't? What you gonna do, huh?"

"Summer!" Karalee shouted.

Spider laughed. "You can call her all you want. Those pills the doctor gave her put her out for the rest of the night."

Karalee picked up the lamp near her bed, holding it in her trembling hand.

Spider narrowed his eyes and pointed his finger at her. "This is a warning. Stop filling Summer's head up with this leaving me bullshit. I ain't going nowhere. This my house. Everything she has belongs to me." He smiled. "That's right. She made me beneficiary over her estate today."

Unable to fully process everything, Karalee shook her head in disbelief. She flipped a tear from her eye.

He smiled wickedly. "Your plan ain't gonna work. I'm here to stay. She loves me." His hands slipped downward covering his male hood. "As long as I keep laying this pipe to her, I ain't going no place."

Karalee looked away in disgust.

He moved away, turning her grandmother's table over before exiting the room.

Once he was gone, Karalee jumped from the bed and locked the door. Her entire body was trembling as she dropped on the bed.

Marcus gave Karalee a warm cup of tea.

"Thank you," Karalee said, taking a sip to calm her nerves. After Spider had confronted her, she'd been a nervous wreck. She'd had no place to go so she'd jumped into her SUV and headed for his place.

"You have to move out of your sister's house," Marcus said, rubbing her back.

"I know," Karalee said, feeing stressed.

Marcus moved in closer. "Why don't you move in with me? I can let my cousin stay in the guesthouse in the back. He's been begging to stay there since he moved in, and you and I can have this place to ourselves."

Karalee felt her stomach twisting from his words. She put her cup on the table, unable to drink it. "I'm not shacking up with you, Marcus. I'm never going down that road again."

"Then let me set you up in your own place," he persisted.

"And let you pay for everything."

"So what?" Marcus eyes went dark.

"I'm getting my own place with my own money."

"If it will make you feel better, you can pay me back," he continued, trying to persuade her.

"I'm still paying you for the truck."

Marcus sat back on the couch, looking stressed. "Why are you being so stubborn? Let me help you help you. That's what a man does when he loves a woman."

Karalee hated to see Marcus upset. She grabbed his hand. "I understand and appreciate what you're trying to do, but I'm saving up money. With the new promotion, I should be out of there soon." She shook her head. "You have to understand what I went through with Chris and how that effected me. When I walked back into our apartment and found out he'd taken everything..." She shook her head unable to finish.

Marcus lifted her face to his." Don't let that incident stop you from letting me help you. What if Spider hurts you?"

Karalee shrugged off the words. "He's just running his mouth."

"Maybe he is, but I won't be able to rest knowing you're there with him."

"Marcus; please." Karalee held up her hand, ending the conversation. "I've made up my mind. Look, don't worry so much. I think I may have found a place."

Marcus eyes lit up. "Really?"

"Yeah, there's a condo on Lane Street. I'm going in tomorrow to see what the requirements are, okay?"

"Alright." Marcus rubbed her back. "I'm not going to stress you out anymore than you already are. Just, please tell me you'll stay with me tonight."

Karalee nodded, and he pulled her into his arms.

Later that night, Marcus wandered into the bathroom while Karalee was taking a shower. He was still upset about Spider, and even more troubled that Karalee refused to let him fix this situation. For the life of him, he couldn't understand why she wouldn't accept his help. Why did she have to be so darn stubborn?

His mind emptied when he saw Karalee. He'd only come in to bring her a fresh towel, but the moment he saw her reflection through the stained glass, he turned concrete hard.

Pulling off his tee shirt and jeans, he opened the shower door.

Karalee's eyes widened before they filled with desire.

"Mind if I join you?"

"Are you kidding me? I've been fanaticizing about showering with you since that day you cornered me in this bathroom."

Marcus slipped off his boxers, enjoying the fire in Karalee's eyes.

He grabbed the sponge from her. "Let me do this." He lathered up a good amount of suds and began massaging it all over her body.

"How does that feel?" he asked as he rubbed the sponge over one breast while gently thumbing the other.

Karalee threw her head back. "Good; really good." She moaned when one hand trailed downward, covering her soft spot.

The sound of her sexy voice was Marcus's undoing. He felt his erection straining. Quickly, he rinsed the suds from her flesh. He moved behind. Entering her, he found her slick and hot. Her tightness was so overwhelming, his legs almost buckled.

Slowly, he moved in and out, trying to contain the cry that wanted to tear from his throat. His movements started out controlled and unhurried, but before he realized it, he was going hard and fast. He felt her getting wetter- tighter. And then she began throwing it back to him. He swallowed a scream. Karalee was remarkable! Together they were the perfect fit. She was the lock and he was the key. They were made for each other. He knew he would never love or enjoy another woman over her. He felt her shiver and she called out his name before her legs buckled.

"I got you," he said, kissing her neck. He lifted her back to standing, and reentered her. His body began burning as he moved within her sweetness. The fire stayed contained in his sac for a while, but soon it was spreading throughout his entire body. He experienced an orgasm that blew his mind. Breathless, he wanted to collapse. Instead he helped her from the shower.

He grabbed a towel, drying her off and feeling every part of her body along the way. By the time his hands had touched every part of her body, he was ready again.

He picked her up and carried her to the bedroom. It was going to be a long, satisfying night.

A week later, Karalee sat in her office handling her business. She loved her office and her job. The morning had been busy as usual. Adjusting to such a position wasn't easy, but she made it look simple. This morning she'd spoken with the managing director in Madrid, and had just finished translating a document from Spanish to English. A knock sounded on her opened office door.

"Marcus." she smiled. She was happy to see him even though she'd been with him last night. Tensions between her and Spider were still high, and she didn't like being around him.

Marcus strolled inside, closing the door. "I came to ask a pretty lady if she'd like to go out to lunch with me."

"I'd love to go," Karalee said, switching off her computer. She grabbed her purse. Just as she was about to head for the door, her desk phone began ringing.

The news she received caused her to sit back in her office chair. After the call was over, Karalee hung the phone up in disbelief.

"I can't believe it," she said, forgetting everything else.

"What's wrong?" Marcus asked, already at her side.

"Nothing's wrong. In fact everything's good. I got the apartment."

"But I thought you said they'd turned down your application?"

"Yeah, but the property manager said there was a mistake with my paperwork. I was approved."

"Congratulations!" Marcus took her into his arms, lifting her from the floor.

"I can't believe it." Karalee wrapped her arms around his neck and return the kiss he gave her. "I did it. I really did it."

"We'll celebrate over lunch," Marcus said, putting her safely back onto the floor.

As they moved out of her office, Karalee experienced a sense of pride she'd never felt. She was doing things on her own and would be completely Independent once she signed her lease. All of her dreams were finally coming true.

Lunch was a two hour celebration of good food, rich deserts and nonstop drinks. Marcus went all out to celebrate the special milestone in Karalee's life. After lunch they would head to her apartment. Karalee had already seen it once, but she was anxious to look at her new home again.

Karalee threw her napkin onto the center of her empty plate. "I may be too full to concentrate when we get back to work."

"Who said we were going back to work?" Marcus slid in closer and gave her a wet kiss.

"What have you planned?"

"You and I are taking the rest of the day off."

"Really?"

"Yes. We're going furniture shopping."

Karalee sighed. "Marcus, I'm buying my own furniture piece by piece."

"I understand you want to be Ms. Independent, but can't a guy buy his lady a housewarming present?"

Karalee let out a sigh. She was about to say something else when she noticed Marcus's attention was diverted. At first she thought he was looking at the beautiful woman at the table next to theirs, but then she noticed his eyes were trained on a little boy, sitting at the table who was crying.

The little boy had spilled his drink and the woman was yelling at him. She snatched the child up from the table and pressed her fingers into his tiny shoulders, shaking him.

Karalee was shocked by the women's behavior and some of the words she called the child. Still, she decided to turn her attention back to their table. But Marcus continued to look. His eyes were dilated and burning with fury.

Karalee asked him if he was he okay, but he was so engrossed in what was happening at the table that he didn't hear her.

Unexpectedly, Marcus stood from his seat and thundered to the table.

"Hey; what's your problem! Get your hands off of him!" he shouted at the woman.

"Excuse you." The woman stared at him like he had three heads.

"He's just a little boy. So what he spill juice on his clothes? It was an accident. You don't have to talk to him like that?"

"Mind your own business!" The woman shouted. She snatched the little boy's hand and moved away.

Shocked by Marcus's explosion, Karalee moved to him. "Marcus, what are you doing?"

He blinked and focused on her. Still, he looked completely out of it.

"She had no right treating that kid like that," he muttered, running his hand across his low cut hair.

She thought she saw tears in his eyes, but he looked away before she could confirm it. "Maybe we should leave." Karalee suggested.

"I agree," he said, moving to get his things from the table. They exited the restaurant in silence.

***

Karalee decided to let Marcus cool down. The ride to her new apartment was silent. By the time he moved into her condo, he had brightened up some.

"This place is nice," he said, shaking his head.

"The manager said they will be renovating the entire complex over the next few months. Mines is the first that will be refurbished"

"That's good," Marcus said.

"I love the kitchen," Karalee said, running her hand across the smooth countertop.

"And the bedrooms are spacious," Marcus added. "Plus, you have plenty of closet space."

He stopped and faced her. "So when will you be moving in?"

"This weekend," She grabbed his hand and they moved onto the patio. "I don't have much to move in except my clothes and my grandmother's table."

"And the new kitchen, living room and bedroom set I'm buying you."

Karalee was about to tell him no, but he put his hand over her mouth and shushed her. "It's not up for discussion."

"What about what happened at the restaurant?" Karalee asked. "Is that up for discussion?"

Silent, Marcus sat on the ledge. His eyes trailed over the huge compound.

"Why were you so upset?" Karalee continued to probe.

"Because the same thing happened to me."

"What are you talking about?" Karalee asked, feeling her heart rate increase.

He focused his teary eyes on her. "When I was little boy I was abused."

"Abused?"

"Yes; verbally?"

Karalee couldn't hold in her gasp.

He looked straight ahead. "I didn't tell you the full story about my mother."

"Was she the one who verbally abused you?" Karalee asked, sitting next to him.

"No; God no. My mother was a very good woman. She was a fighter and had an outspoken personality just like you." He stroked her chin before his eyes darkened. "Her only fault was she trusted my father too much. In her eyes he could do no wrong. She didn't know that he'd been having an affair and had father six kids with his mistress. She took it hard the day she found out. She had a heart attack. A few days later she died."

Karalee listened in horror as he continued.

"A month after mom died, dad married his mistress, Margret. My mother's body wasn't even cold in the grave and he moved Margret and their children into the home they'd shared." His hands were shaking and tears raced down his face. "That woman got rid of all my mother's things and redecorated. I wanted to kill her."

Karalee rested her head on his chest, listening to his words along with the pounding of his heart.

"After Margret moved in, dad would go out of town on so called business trips. Really, he was still seeing multiple women. He'd be gone for days…sometimes weeks, leaving us alone with her." He shook his head. "Margret was so mean. She would feed her children first. We would have to eat last. And the things she said about mom…"

Karalee found some tissue for him to wipe his face.

"It was terrible." He dried his face but more tears rolled out. "I got treated the worst. Margret would punish me for protecting my brothers and sister. One time, we were in the kitchen, and I accidently broke one of her favorite's glasses. She ordered me to clean it up. I guess I wasn't moving fast enough because she shoved me. I slipped and landed on the floor on top of the glass. I had to have stitches and my side was scarred badly."

"That's why you have the tattoo," Karalee whispered.

He nodded.

"But why didn't you tell somebody?"

"I never trusted anyone enough to."

Karalee was humbled that he'd trusted in her enough to tell her about such a devastating past. Still, she was troubled. "What about your dad? Why didn't you tell him?"

"Margret had convinced my dad that I was the problem. She got into his head. He believed her over us. That's when I started to rebel. I was so angry I would fight at school. Dad made the decision to send me to a private school in another state. I had to leave my sister and brothers. It hurt like hell not being able to protect them, but thank God my aunt had stepped in by then to get them. I stayed in the private school for three years. My stepmom was happy. She thought she was punishing me, but it actually ended up being the best thing to happen to me."

"How so?"

"I met my boxing instructor there. He became like a father figure to me. He taught me how to box to release my anger."

"That's why you opened the gym?"

"Yeah. I know how it feels to be young and have grown ass people pick on you. I know what it feels like to feel angry…hopeless. People thought that we were happy just because dad had lots of money, but we were miserable."

Karalee rubbed his back and kissed away his tears.

"What happened to your dad?"

"He got sick. He had a stroke twice. He's learning how to talk and walk all over again. I see him from time to time, but not as much as I should."

"Why not?"

"Because he's still married to Margret and every time I see her…." He shook his head.

"It brings up bad memories."

He nodded. "And I've come too far with controlling my anger to turn back."

"Marcus, you can't be silent about this. There are so many children and teens going through the same thing. A man in your position can help spread awareness."

He looked hesitant. "I'm not ready to open up to the world about this, Karalee. Maybe one day, but for now my gym is my way to help."

Karalee laced her hand with his. "I understand. Mr. Tucker." She kissed him. "Did anyone ever tell you what a wonderful, amazing man you are?"

He smiled. "Yeah, but it never mattered until I heard it from you."

15

A week later, Marcus found Carlos sitting on the couch looking dejected. Upon approaching him, he noticed his eyes were fire red.

"Carlos; what's wrong, man?"

"Like you'd care," Carlos snapped, turning away from him.

"I do care." Marcus sat on the couch next to him. "You're my cousin." He placed a hand his leg. "Come on, tell me what happened."

Carlos turned to him and dropped his head. "Kiki broke up with me," he muttered.

"Why?"

"She started messing with another boy on the football team."

Marcus dropped his head and shook it.

"I couldn't spend time with her because I had to work. Thanks to you." Carlos muttered that part under his breath. "

Marcus had heard. He looked at him. "I only want the best for you, Carlos. It was not my intention to make you lose time with your friends or girlfriend. I just want to teach you how to be responsible and a man of your word." He patted his shoulder. "I know you may not want to hear this, but you will get over Kiki. You will be okay."

Marcus cell phone started ringing. It was Emily. He was already late for their meeting.

"I'll pick you up from school today. We'll talk later, okay?"

Carlos didn't respond or even look at him.

Marcus patted his shoulder again. He would surprise him later. He planned to leave work early and spend time talking with him man to man.

A half hour later, Carlos ended up in Marcus's garage. He loved the flashy cars, and the Harley-Davidson was off the chain! He thought about Kiki again. She was the first girl he'd really like. He was actually getting serious with her. Now she was with Mike, the guy who'd befriended him his first day at the academy. He didn't want to go to school again and see them together. Tensions were sure to be high being he and Mike were on the same football team.

He sat on the Harley Davidson motorcycle and played with it for a while. He wanted to get out and go for a ride on it. Even though he had never driven a motorcycle, he was sure it wouldn't be much harder than driving a car. Moving upstairs, he found the place Marcus kept all of the keys.

He headed back to the garage and grabbed a helmet. He would be back before Marcus came home. He'd never find out. He started the Harley Davidson and revved up the engine.

Soon he was moving slowly down the road with the sun on his back, and the wind caressing his face.

Operating the motorcycle was easier than he'd thought. Deciding he could handle the bike, he sped up. He felt better already. He thought about going to Kiki's house and showing off. Maybe she would regret breaking up with him if she saw him on a bike like this. Yes, he would do that.

He approached a curve and tried to slow down, but he lost control. Suddenly he was flying through the air. He felt his body land against the pavement and searing pain before everything went dark.

Marcus was in the middle of a meeting with Emily when he was interrupted by his new personal assistant, Rebecca.

"Mr. Tucker you have a very important call." Rebecca said, moving into the conference room.

He stood from the table and looked at Rebecca. She was coming along nicely with the job, but she certainly couldn't perform on Karalee's level. Still, he was nice and patient with her. But his patience was running thin at the moment. He'd told her not to interrupt him from his meeting unless it was a life or death situation. He reminded her of that now.

"Sir, I'm afraid it is a life or death situation."

Marcus excused himself from the curious glances from his employees and took the cell phone. He almost dropped the phone when he heard the news.

Marcus tried to process everything that was going on. But it was too much to take in. Too much to digest. Carlos had been in a bad accident on his motorcycle. By the time he, his brothers and sister arrived, Carlos was already in surgery. For eight hours, he sat anxiously in the waiting room with his family. His heart pounded with fear the entire time.

When Dr. Walker entered the waiting room, his face didn't look good. The family immediately gathered around him.

"He nearly lost his leg," Dr. Walker revealed. "His left knee was severely dislocated. He had three torn ligaments and no blood flow to his foot. He now has rods holding his knee in place. You're lucky he got to the hospital on time. He'll never play football again, and we are still not sure if he'll ever be able to walk on that left leg. Only time will tell. But he's lucky to have both of his legs. He will have to stay in the hospital until he can at least use crutches. He has a long road of recovery ahead of him."

Marcus dropped his head. He felt crushed and devastated. Carlos had been hurt while in his care. That was the last thing he wanted.

"This is not your fault," Emily and his brothers told him as they rallied around him.

Marcus wished he felt the same. He should have stayed and talked to Carlos after he'd told him about the breakup with Kiki, then this wouldn't have happened. He promised himself that he was going to make sure his cousin received the best treatments possible.

Later that night, when Carlos woke up, Marcus broke the news to him. Carlos turned his head away from him and told him to leave the room.

"Get out!" he screamed. "I don't want to see you again!"

Marcus was completely hurt and confused, but he didn't want to upset Carlos any further, so he obeyed his wishes.

Karalee sealed the last box. She sat on the bed once she was done and sighed. She was worried about Marcus. It had been a week since his cousin's accident and he was still in the dumps. Marcus had spent most of his time at the hospital despite what Carlos had told him about never coming back to see him. Daily, he visited and checked on his progress.

Karalee tried to convince him that it wasn't his fault that the accident had occurred, but Marcus continued to feel responsible. She stayed by him and supported him during the difficult time. She prayed Carlos would walk again, and that Marcus would heal, and not feel guilty.

Karalee looked at the boxes again that she'd packed. She only had two boxes of things that belonged to her. At least she had her grandmother's table. Marcus had even brought her some very nice furniture that would be delivered tomorrow morning. She had refused, but he wouldn't hear of it. He said the furniture were housewarming presents from him.

Summer knocked on the opened basement door.

"I'm glad to see you're up." Karalee smiled.

"I feel almost back to normal," Summer said, sitting on her bed. "So your moving into you own apartment?"

Karalee nodded proudly.

"Are you sure you're ready? Why the rush?"

The incident between her and Spider flashed before her eyes, but Karalee didn't bother to tell Summer. She would side with Spider anyway. "I've overstayed my welcome," she said instead.

"If it's because of the things I said; I want to apologize."

"It has nothing to do with that," Karalee cut her off. "I'm not mad at you. I just wash my hands. I love you. But I learned my lesson. I'm staying out of you and Spider's business."

Summer dropped her head. "Well, this room is yours if you need to move back in."

"I love being with you, but I don't think so," Karalee laughed.

The two sisters hugged.

"Take care of yourself." Karalee squeezed her tighter.

"I will," Summer said, pulling back and wiping her eyes.

"I don't know what I'd do if something happens to you."

"Nothing's gonna happen to me," Summer fussed. "I mean, you're just moving a few miles away. I'll visit you and you can visit me."

"I'm checking on you every day." Karalee promised.

"Yeah right; you'll be so caught up with Marcus Tucker that I probably won't see you."

"How did you know about me and Marcus?" Karalee asked, shocked.

"Girl please. I knew it would happen. You're lucky to have him and he's damn lucky to have you."

Karalee smiled. She stood from the bed and collected a box. "How about you come over for dinner once I'm settled in."

"It's a deal," Summer said. "As long as you let me cook."

The two sisters laughed as they exited the basement room.

16

The next month passed swiftly for Marcus. Carlos had been released from the hospital. He moved in with Emily. Marcus made sure he received the best treatments, and that he had the best doctors. It hurt Marcus that his cousin didn't want to see him, but he prayed time would change his mind.

The bright spot in his life was Karalee. He'd helped her settle into her new apartment. She was thriving in her new position with Tucker Insurance too. Due to her, he hadn't sunk into a terrible depression over Carlos.

Any free time he had was spent with her. They took turns staying at each other's places. No matter where they resided, they had fun. They worked, played, and shared everything. The nights always ended with lovemaking. Karalee always fall asleep on his chest, wrapped in his arms.

Marcus couldn't believe he'd found a woman who pleased him fully. He was completely in love with her and admired her as a woman.

This Saturday afternoon, he followed Karalee into his home. The day had been busy. He'd visited his sister Emily's house to check on Carlos. Afterwards, he and Karalee had popped in on the set where the new Tucker

Insurance commercial was being shot. Then they'd traveled to the gym. Now his muscles were aching. He wanted to relax for the night with the woman he loved.

"Why don't we take a shower together?" Marcus asked while he planted kisses on her neck.

"Oh, I'd love that." Karalee smiled, kicking off her shoes. "I've been lusting after you all day."

Instantly he felt his arousal. He tried to pull her in his arms and take her then, but she moved away. "Let me put these files in your upstairs office first, baby."

"Hurry up," Marcus ordered, while rubbing his massive hands together and watching her switch away.

He headed for the shower and was soon under the spray of warm water. What's taking her so long, he thought. He heard his cell and turned the shower off. It could be Emily. He had to answer it. He was paranoid something would happen to Carlos. He wanted to be there if it did.

Dripping wet, he stepped outside onto the mat. He grabbed his towel and began drying off some. He reached for his phone. It was the real estate agency.

"Hi Marcus," his agent Terri said cheerily into the line. "I just faxed over the closing documents for the apartment complex."

Marcus felt his heart in his throat. He quickly thanked Terri and reached for the towel. Why did she send the papers now of all times? Karalee was upstairs in his home office.

Just as he was about to head out, the bathroom door opened.

From the look on Karalee's face he knew everything was out. "Do you want to explain this?" she asked, waving the papers at him. "I should have known," she tossed the documents at him.

"Karalee; baby wait!" He followed her out of the bathroom. He grabbed her hand. "I was only trying to help you."

"By going behind my back and buying my condo?"

"You wouldn't let me help you. I was scared, okay? When they turned down your application, I didn't want you to continue staying at your sister's house around Spider, so I...I purchased the apartment complex. I mean, all I wanted to do was help you. What was I supposed to do?"

"Let me do it by myself!" she shouted. She shook her head. "You don't get it, do you, Marcus? I wanted to find my own way. I wanted to see if I could do this by myself and you took that away from me. You had no right!"

He watched helplessly as she snatched up her purse.

He tried to grab her, but she swiftly averted him and moved out the door.

He called out after her several times, but she ignored him.

He grabbed the first clothes he could find. He threw them on and went after her.

***

Later that night, Marcus returned home. He was defeated and depressed. He had searched all over for Karalee, but she was nowhere to be found. He'd had no idea the real estate company would fax over the remaining documents today? Or that Karalee would find them upstairs still in his fax machine. He sat on the couch kneading his tired eyes. He just wanted to fix everything…protect her.

He let out a weary sigh. Maybe Karalee was right. He should have let her do things by herself. But love had forced him to step in and intervene. He only wanted the best for her.

His cell phone began ringing. His heart jumped into his throat at the possibility that it might be Karalee. His disappointment soared when he saw it was his sister.

"Emily, Is Carlos okay?"

"He's fine. I need you to get over here, ASAP."

"What's going on?"

"I'm not discussing this over the phone. You'd better get over to my place quick."

The urgency in her voice alarmed him.

He dragged his hands down his face. Whatever news Emily had couldn't be any worse than what he had experienced earlier. Of that he was he was sure.

***

Karalee avoided Marcus on Sunday. She'd stay at the motel the night before. She knew her apartment would be the first place he'd look for her. She debated half the night on what she should do. She shut off her phone and tried to think. Maybe she was being bullheaded, but Marcus shouldn't have done what he had. She'd been so proud of herself. She'd thought she'd finally done something on her own. Knowing he'd went behind her back and purchased that apartment complex took that pride away.

She knew the situation was nothing to throw a relationship away over, but he had to respect her decision to be independent and do things on her own.

Now she was at Summer's house seated in front of a plate of mouth-watering Sunday dinner that she couldn't eat.

"Do you know how silly you sound?" Summer asked after Karalee shared what had happened yesterday.

"How is what I shared silly?" Karalee asked, confused by Summer's sudden shift in mood.

"You're mad because Marcus went behind your back and brought that condo for you. So what? Do you know how many women wished they had a man who supported them like that?" Summer stood and grabbed her plate and thundered away.

"Why are you mad?" Karalee followed.

"Because I don't get it."

"Get what?"

"How a woman like you, who don't appreciate blessings, get them." Tears were in her eyes as she leaned on the counter and stared at her.

"Do you know how lucky you are to have him, Karalee? Do you have any idea how hard I've tried to make my man do right? I have to beg him to get a job to help take care of me…his kids?"

"Summer-"

"No; shut up and listen." Summer held up her hand. "You've got a perfect, successful guy who loves you. You will never find another man like that; I promise you. That man will do anything to take care of you, and you're selfish and unappreciative. And why? Because you're scared he's going to do you like Chris did. Please grow up. So what Chris left you and took all of your shit. Get over it and move on before you lose him." Summer threw the dishrag down and thundered out of the kitchen.

Karalee stood in a state of stupor for a few minutes. Summer's words had been like a slap to the face. A slap she needed. She grabbed her purse and headed for the door. Tomorrow she would have a long heart to heart talk with Marcus. Things had to change, and she knew it would have to start with her.

***

Karalee tried for the third time to unlock her office door. She looked at her key. It was the key to her office. So why wouldn't it open? She gave up and moved to Marcus's office for answers. She had to talk with him anyway. She wanted to talk with him after work. But it appeared it would have to be now. She heard elevated voices as she knocked on his partly opened door. The door opened fully and Val stood in view.

"Mr. Tucker has been waiting on you," Val said, stepping aside and letting her come in.

Upon entering, she noticed two security guards and a very pretty middle aged woman. What struck her as odd was not the pretty woman or even the security guards inside who all seemed to be gawking at her, but Marcus and the dejected look on his face. It was a look she'd never seen before. Even when he'd discussed his stepmother his face hadn't looked so angry-so hurt. He wouldn't even focus on her completely. His eyes would look in her direction briefly before moving away to the other people inside the room. She was about to ask him what was going on when the pretty, middle aged woman who introduced herself as Emily approached her, and told her to have a seat.

Karalee looked at Marcus. Again his clouded eyes refused to remain focused on her.

"Marcus…what's going on?" She asked, feeling a terrible ache in the pit of her stomach.

Marcus looked at her. She thought she saw tears in his eyes.

"I have something very important to ask you, and I hope this is not true," he said, folding his hands together like he was about to say a prayer.

"Your company's credit card was drained," Emily interjected, before Marcus could finish.

Karalee shook her head. "I'm not following you."

"We have statements. You drained your credit card by purchasing personal items."

Karalee looked at Marcus. Her heart was pounding out of her chest. "I would never do anything like that. Marcus you know me."

"Does he? Emily asked, slamming a file on the desk before Karalee.

"What do you mean by that?"

"You've done this before, haven't you?"

"No," Karalee stuttered.

"Oh really?" Emily asked, opening the folder. "When you were eighteen you served six months in prison for credit card fraud."

Karalee felt all the blood rush to her head. For a moment she thought she would pass out. "Marcus, I…I can explain that," she stuttered, flipping tears away from her eyes.

Marcus dropped his head and shook it. "So it's true?"

"Yes; I was in prison, but I didn't misuse my company credit card. It's locked in my office desk. I never touched it. I swear-"

"How could you not tell me you'd been in prison?" Marcus asked. His voice was filled with hurt.

Tears dropped from Karalee's eyes. She was about to explain to him the real reason why she'd been in prison, but Emily interjected.

"My concern is bigger than her not telling you about her past, Marcus. My concern is the missing money." Emily walked in front of her with her arms folded and began chastising her. "Use of corporate credit card for your own personal needs is credit card fraud. Being you violated the terms of our policy, you are terminated.

"Terminated?" Karalee whispered in disbelief.

Marcus stood from his seat and moved to the window.

"We will need the keys to the company car as well as your company credit card."

With trembling hands, Karalee retrieved the keys to the company car. "The credit card is in my desk," she muttered through trembling lips.   She walked to Marcus's desk. He was still facing the window and refused to look at her. Her heart felt like someone had snatched it out and stomped on it. "Here's the key to your apartment too. I don't need anything from you, and I damn sure wouldn't steal from you!"

The two security guards approached her. There was no need for that. Karalee stumbled out of the office, barely able to see from the tears clouding her eyes.

***

"I want everyone to leave," Marcus muttered. "Get out!" Quickly everyone scurried from his office. Only Emily remained. A look of pity was etched on her face as she walked to him.

"I'm so sorry, Marcus."

Marcus's face snapped up and a hot tear rolled down his cheek. Quickly, he wiped it away. He dropped in his office chair, kneading his teary eyes with the heels of his hands. "I don't believe this, Emily."

Emily rested a hand on his shoulder. "Look, Marcus; you can have your opinions in one hand, and your thoughts in the other, but in my hands is the truth." She slammed the folder on the table. "She's a thief." She let out a sigh. "I'm glad someone emailed me the criminal information about her, or I would have never known. I don't understand how she was hired. A full investigation will be conducted."

Marcus dropped his hands and shook his head. "But you…you don't understand," he stuttered in a voice choked with tears. "She wouldn't take anything from me. She wouldn't even let me help her get an apartment."

"Oh Marcus; you are in complete denial."

"No." Marcus shook his head.

"It was all a game to win your trust," Emily continued. "Then she would have taken you for everything you have just like your last girlfriend did. Just be glad I found out. It will save you from a lot of heartache further down the road."

With all the strength Marcus had in his body, he brought his hands down to the desk, causing most of the things on top to fall off. "No! Something's not right. I can't...won't believe this!" he shouted.

Emily looked at him like he was crazy. "What has this woman done to you? What kind of hold does she have on you?"

More tears escaped Marcus's eyes. "I trust her, Emily...I love her."

Emily's eyes grew wide. "I'm calling your brother Jayden to come up here to talk some sense into you," she said, quickly pulling out her cell phone.

Marcus snatched up his car keys. "I have to get out of here," he said before he thundered out of the office, ignoring Emily who was calling for him.

***

Karalee was so confused and hurt, she could only cry. At the motel she sat on the bed feeling completely numb. She had the hotel room for another three days. But after that, where in the hell would she go? She had nothing. Her entire world had been destroyed in seconds, and it was all because of a lie or a glitch. There had to be a mistake in the system. She'd been so careful with that credit Card. She'd always left it secured and locked in her desk.

She lay on the bed with Snow White. Her past came flooding back, and she was forced to face the ugliest. True, she had been in prison for committing credit card fraud, but she had only done it to protect her mother. She had not told Marcus the remainder of the story about her mother and what had happened after her grandmother had died.

She thought about how she'd found her mother on the streets, homeless and selling herself just to get high. Against Summer's advice, she had moved her mother into her grandmother's house. She'd nursed her mother back to health. Her mother had promised she would go to rehab, so Karalee let her remain in the home. Months later, the police came knocking on her door. Someone had used her deceased grandmother's credit cards and had racked up a huge debt. She found out her mother was guilty, but she couldn't let her mother take the fall. Her mother had been in and out of jail for most of her life. A previous judge had told her mother, if she ever came into his courtroom again, he would make sure she did some serious time; so Karalee had taken the blame. She'd said goodbye to her college scholarship and had been sentence to six months, thanks to her lawyer. She'd had to sell the house her grandmother had left her, and spend the insurance money that would have helped her out during college to get the lawyer. But it had been worth it being she hadn't done more time.

She blinked away the tears. Her entire life had been destroyed because of her mother. Now it seemed like her past had come again to bite her in the ass. She was a lot of things, but there was one thing she wasn't: a thief. To know Marcus thought of her in that way hurt her the most. She knew she could not explain this to him. He believed his sister. It was evident when he'd turned his back on her. Curling up on the bed, she cried herself to sleep.

A half hour later, her cell phone roused her. She looked at the caller display. Someone from an area code in Florida was calling.

"Karalee?"

She almost dropped the phone. "Mama…"

17

For the next week, Marcus tried to contact Karalee. It killed him not knowing where she was or if she was safe. During that time, he hired a private investigator to look into the credit card incident. He knew in his heart that Karalee had not done such a thing and he wanted to prove it.

Tonight, he gathered with his family at his sister Emily's house. He wanted to be alone, but it was his nephew's first birthday.

Marcus took a sip of his drink and forced conversations and smiles with his family. The birthday party was action filled. Still, he was in the dumps about Karalee and also Carlos, who was in his room and refused to come out as long as he was there.

Emily distracted his trouble thoughts by pushing out a birthday cake fit for a prince.

Marcus joined his family who was singing happy birthday to, Ford Tucker Jr., the youngest member of the Tucker family. The child was his brother's son and today it was his first birthday. Marcus shook his head and jokingly stuffed his fingers in his ears. "Please everyone." He held up his hands. "No offense, but you people can't sing." The room erupted in laughter. "Why don't we let my beautiful nieces, Angel and Claire sing?"

Claire grabbed Angel's hand. They moved to the middle of the room and began singing happy birthday. Their parents, Ford and Maya, proudly looked on. Everyone clapped when they were done. Marcus kissed his pretty nieces and handsome nephew on the cheek.

Marcus watched the little one who was in his highchair, making a mess with his cake. "I can't believe how big he's gotten," he said.

His brother Ford wrapped an arm around his shoulder. "Well, if you would visit more often instead of spending all of your time at the gym, you wouldn't miss out on so much."

"You need to visit my gym, bro." Marcus teased. "Married life has caused you to put on extra weight."

"What?" Ford flexed the budging muscles in his arm. "Me and you in your boxing ring any day."

"You mean to tell me you'd actually break away from Maya to spar with me?"

"Hey, he's free to do whatever he likes," Maya kissed Ford on the lips. "And for the record, my husband has not put on weight. He's still just as fine as he was the first day we met."

Ford blushed and smiled.

Marcus shook his head as he watched the happy couple move away.

Emily walked beside him. "Someday some woman is going to have you blushing the same way." she interjected.

Marcus instantly thought about Karalee and depression set in.

Emily rubbed his shoulder. "You really need to forget about Karalee."

"I don't want to talk about it," Marcus muttered. He still believed Karalee was innocent. He wasn't about to let his sister talk trash about her.

"Well, can we at least talk about dad's birthday that's coming up?"

"Gladly," Marcus answered, happy for the conversation shift.

"I'm having dad's party at my place this year."

"Is Margret coming?"

"Of course; she's dad's wife."

"Then you can count me out."

"Come on, dad wants all of his sons there."

"Dad can't say more than ten words. This is your idea."

"Okay; so it is. But it's time for you to move on. Margret is not the same woman. She's changed."

"Changed? There's no way a woman that evil can change."

"How would you know? You haven't talked to her in years. It's time to forgive her."

"Forgive her? I wouldn't spit on her if she was on fire."

Emily's eyes widened. "Marcus, that's terrible. You're filled with hate. I'll tell you what, hitting those boxing bags will never give you true peace. Only forgiveness can do that." She shook her head and moved away.

Marcus placed his glass down. "You can talk about forgiveness so easily, can't you?" He followed her. "You didn't have to go through what I did. I protected you all from her."

Emily gave him a flippant wave before she moved into the kitchen, ignoring him. He moved away and kissed his nephew and nieces goodbye. He didn't want to hear about forgiveness, especially from someone who hadn't walked in his shoes.

"So not only are you moving back in with me, but you're bringing mama too?" Summer asked Karalee as they walked into the basement.

Karalee dropped the box of things she'd brought for her mother onto the bed. "Listen, mama needs me. She needs us. She's real sick. She wants to come here and get better."

Summer shook her head. "How many years has mama been telling you and me that?" Summer sucked her teeth. "You went to prison for her and she still didn't change her ways. What makes you think she will change now?"

"I'm not giving up on mama."

"But you'll give up on everyone else."

"What do you mean by that?" Karalee asked, removing some of the clothes from the box and folding them.

"Marcus has been to my house twice looking for you. Call the man and talk to him. Tell him what really happened, and why you were in prison."

"I plan to do that, but right now, I need to get things straight for mama. Her train is arriving this afternoon."

"And how did she get money for a train?"

"I sent it to her."

Summer laughed. "When will you learn? That money is already gone up in smoke. Mama is never gonna change."

Marcus heard the doorbell. He opened the door and welcomed in Travis, the detective he'd hired to look into the missing money from the credit card.

"I hope you have some answers for me," Marcus said, offering him a seat.

"I have answers, but I'm not sure you're gonna like them."

"What do you mean by that?" Marcus asked, anxiously sitting on the edge of the sofa.

Travis powered on his lap top and slipped in a disk.

Marcus felt his heart aching as he looked at the computer. Images came into view.

"Mr. Tucker, your assumptions were correct."

"What do you mean?" Marcus asked, looking closely at the image on the screen. The only thing he saw was what looked like a jewelry store.

"Do you recognize this lady?"

Marcus felt his heart stall in his chest when the woman came into focus.

He nodded. "Yes, I know her, but what does she have to do with this?"

"She's the person who used Karalee's credit card."

Marcus was in a confused state for a moment. The anger set in. He balled his fist and hit his hand. "I should have known," he muttered. He couldn't believe a woman he'd trusted could sink so low. However, it would prove Karalee had told the truth.

"I have more information on Karalee as well," Travis said, pulling out a folder.

By the time Travis had told him all that he had found out about Karalee, Marcus was dizzy.

He shot up from his seat. "Give me a copy of that," he ordered.

Travis nodded and gave Marcus the evidence.

Marcus wasted no time saying goodbye. He led the detective outside and hopped inside his car. He pulled out his cell phone.

"Let me speak to Emily now!" he growled, before screeching off down the road.

***

"Marcus, I don't understand what's going on," Emily said, sitting in the chair across from him inside his office.

"You will understand real soon," he said, flipping on the flat screen television. He pressed the pause button.

There was a light tap on the door.

Val entered.

"Mr. Tucker, you wanted to see me?" Val asked.

"Yes, have a seat."

"What's going on, Mr. Tucker?"

Marcus sat back in his seat. "You tell me."

"What do you mean, sir?" Val laughed uncomfortably.

"Tell me the truth about Karalee's credit card."

"I don't know what you're talking about."

"Neither do I," Emily interjected.

Marcus held up his hand to hush Emily. He leaned forward in his seat. "All I want to know is why? Why'd you do it, Val?"

"Mr. Tucker, are you accusing me of using Karalee's credit card?" Val looked angry.

"No; I'm not accusing you. I know you did it."

"I swear on my mother's grave; I didn't do it."

Marcus dropped his head and let out a sigh. Then he pressed the play button on the remote.

"What is this?" Emily asked.

"Footage of Val buying things using Karalee's credit card."

"How do you know that is Karalee's credit card?" Emily asked.

Marcus zoomed in and the numbers on the credit card showed perfectly.

"Oh my God." Emily shook her head before dropping it.

Marcus paused the recording. "Now all I want to know is how and why?"

Val's lips trembled. "You promoted her.... I was angry," she sobbed. "I didn't know it would go this far."

"How did you get her credit card?"

"I picked the lock on her desk and switched cards with her so she wouldn't notice it was missing."

"And then you drained her card?"

"Yes... I'm sorry," Val continued to sob.

"How could you sink so low, Val?" Emily stared at her in disgust. "You've been with us for ten years. We trusted you and had you at our home for dinner on several occasions."

"I can pay it back."

"It goes deeper than that, Val," Emily muttered. "I have no choice but to terminate you. I expect your things to be cleared from the office before noon."

Val stood, her entire body shaking. She apologized again before leaving the office.

Emily and Marcus both were quiet for a few seconds before Emily spoke. "It was her who sent me that email?"

"Yeah. She found out Karalee had been in prison for similar charges and wanted it to appear as if she'd done the same thing to us."

"But, I don't understand; did Karalee use up her grandmother's credit cards after she died?"

Marcus sighed. For the next ten minutes, he shared everything with Emily that Detective Travis had told him about the true reason why Karalee had gone to prison.

"You truly have an amazing woman, Marcus," Emily said when he was done. "I'm sorry. Please let me apologize to her. Will you bring her to dad's birthday party tomorrow?"

"I don't know if I'm coming, but if I do, I'll think about it." He stood from his desk. "I need to make a run."

"Where are you going?"

"To apologize to the woman I love."

"Once again mama played you." Summer said, shaking her head.

"Maybe she missed her train." Karalee tried to think positive.

"She's not coming." Summer sat on a bench outside of the train station.

"How much money did you send her?"

Karalee was too embarrassed to tell her. "I sent her more than enough," she muttered.

"She used that money to get high."

Karalee's heart was pounding. She tried calling the number her mom had given her, but the cell phone was off.

Feeling like a fool, Karalee followed Summer back to her truck. She had spent money she didn't really have buying an extra bed for the basement room. She'd gotten her mother some clothes and other personal things she would need too.

Once inside her truck, Karalee knocked everything from the dashboard.

Summer hugged her as she sobbed.

"Why does she keep doing this to me?" Karalee cried. "I'm done with her this time. I promise."

"Karalee, you've got to accept the cards we were dealt.

Summer rubbed her back. "I know you want mama to change and be the mother we never had, but that is not gonna happen. You've done all you can to help her. Mama is never gonna be a mother to us. She will never change."

The words stung, but this time Karalee let it hurt and finally accepted the truth.

When Karalee pulled into the driveway, she saw Marcus's SUV. A flood of emotions took over. She felt everything from anger to excitement at seeing him. Seeing him made her realize how much she really missed and loved him."

"Talk to him," Summer said, before speaking and moving away.

Karalee moved outside of her truck and folded her arms across her chest, watching as Marcus approached her.

"What are you doing here?"

"Would you mind taking a ride with me? I want to talk to you."

"About what? The fact that you think I'm a thief?"

He grabbed her wrist and pulled her close. "I never believed you did those things, Karalee."

"Well, it sure didn't appear that way when we at your office. I would never take anything from you or anyone else."

"I know. That's why I'm here. I want to apologize."

"Why didn't you stand up for me in front of your sister?"

"I didn't know what to think. I needed to sort things out so I could present the facts to my sister and the board. I had to clear your name."

"What are you talking about?"

"I hired a private investigator."

"And?"

Marcus watched the emotions play on Karalee's face as he told her everything that he'd discovered. When he was done, he noticed anger mixed with tears in her eyes.

"I knew Val was evil, but I can't believe she went through all of that to set me up."

"Well, she's no longer employed with the company," he said. "What she did is reprehensible. What I don't understand is why you didn't tell me you went to prison for your mother?"

Karalee shook her head. "I was embarrassed."

"Sweetie, you shouldn't have been embarrassed to tell me that. It wouldn't have changed my love for you. You are one hell of a woman, Karalee."

She didn't pull away when he hugged her. She'd missed him and she still loved him. He kissed her forehead and before she knew it they were lip to lip, kissing like they were in private.

Marcus broke the kiss and stroked her chin. "Can we please get out of here?" he asked breathless.

Karalee could only moan her response.

By the time the door closed to Marcus's Triplex home, he had Karalee in his arms. Upstairs, he headed to his room. He was painfully aroused. Swiftly he tore at her clothes, not caring where they landed. He placed her naked body onto his bed. He lay beside her.

"Damn, I missed you," he said, planting sweet kisses across her body.

"I missed you too," she said, wrapping her arms tightly around his back.

"Show me how much," he said, pulling her top.

When her tongue pushed into his mouth, he weakened and his nature jerked.

In no time he entered her, finding her hot and wet. He would not be easy. Maybe later, but being deprived of her for so long had him feeling animalistic.

She was just as needy as him, matching each thrust with her own. When he heard her scream out his name, heat began burning in his lower body. He knew he could not hold out much longer. In and out he moved, loving the fire that was slowly building. Trembling, he lost the last bit of control he had. Fire spread throughout his entire body and left him speechless. For the next few seconds, his body shook with shudder after shudder as pleasure overtook him.

Later that night, Marcus made love to Karalee again. The loving was so intense it put them both in a deep sleep. When Marcus woke up a few hours later, they showered together and sat on his patio, enjoying the cool wind.

He grabbed her hand and kissed it. "Karalee, I need to apologize."

"Marcus, please stop apologizing. I forgive you?"

He held up his hand. "I want to apologize for going behind your back and buying that condo. You're right. I shouldn't have done that. It's just that...damnit, I love you so much. I just wanted to help you-protect you, but you're right, I have to respect your wishes to do things on your own and be independent. "

Karalee put her hand to his lips and shushed him.

"I appreciate all that you have done to try to help me. Don't ever think I didn't."

Marcus kissed her nose. "The job and apartment is still yours, if you'll accept it," he said. "If you don't, "I'll understand."

Karalee nodded and Marcus pulled her into his arms. "What are you doing tomorrow night?"

"Hopefully spending the night with you." Karalee smiled.

"I'm going to my father's birthday party."

"Really?"

"Yes."

"But won't your stepmother be there?"

"Yeah, but I think I can handle it with you there to support me."

Karalee's eyes widened in surprise. "You want me to come with you?"

"Yes; I want to introduce my family to the woman I love."

Karalee looked up at him with surprise etched on her face.

"I'd love to meet your family."

18

The next night Karalee tried to keep her mouth shut when Marcus escorted her into his sister's beautiful mansion.

She tried to breathe as they moved into the main area. Marcus introduced her to his four brothers, six half brothers and brother-in-law Stanley. They were all just as handsome as him. Karalee felt lightheaded being surrounded by so many good-looking men who were all complimenting her. The Tuckers were a wonderful family! They were very friendly and made her feel right at home.

A beautiful woman, with red hair, who introduced herself as Maya interrupted them.

"Do you mind if I borrow her for a few minutes?" Maya asked, grabbing Karalee's hand.

"Don't keep her too long," Marcus ordered playfully, before kissing Karalee on the lips.

Karalee took a deep breath and followed Maya to the party area. There were a variety of cocktail tables, but both decided on a refreshing glass of punch.

"So how are you holding up?" Maya asked, guiding her outside onto the balcony.

"I'm nervous," Karalee admitted.

"So was I the first time I met the family." She laughed. "Just take a deep breath and enjoy yourself, hon."

Before she could thank her, she felt a hand on her back. She turned and was face to face with Emily. Maya and Emily gave each other a hug and cheek kiss before Maya left them alone.

"Emily grabbed her free hand and squeezed it as they walked further onto the balcony. "I want you to know that I'm very sorry about everything that took place."

"There's no need to apologize."

Emily held up a hand. "Oh believe me, you deserve an apology. So when will you be returning back to work?"

"Monday."

"That's great. I think you're doing an excellent job, and you're making my brother extremely happy."

Karalee felt her heart pumping. "He's making me very happy too."

"Welcome to the family." Emily gave her a tight hug.

When she pulled away, Karalee stared at her curiously. "What do you mean?"

Emily smiled. "I have a feeling you will be a Tucker in the very near future."

Emily kissed her cheek and moved away, leaving Karalee flabbergasted. Before she could fully digest the words, she felt a hand wrap around her waist and smooth lips connect with her neck.

"Hey, are you okay?"

She turned to Marcus and linked an arm around his waist, "I'm happy…very happy," Karalee smiled, blinking away tears as he guided her back into the huge room.

Marcus saw the monster as soon as he and Karalee stepped back inside the house.

He'd been calling his stepmom, Margret, that since the day his father, Michael, had married her. His body shook as he watched her move in, pushing his father in a wheel chair. She'd aged some, but she still looked the same. Her skin was fair, her hair blonde, and her eyes crystal blue. Marcus hated those eyes. He hated everything about her.

He shuttered in anger. "I don't think I can stay here," he muttered.

"Yes, you can." Karalee squeezed his hand.

Marcus moved to his father and gave him a hug, before introducing him to Karalee. His dad's voice was slurry and slow. Still, he managed to tell Karalee that it was nice to meet her. Marcus rubbed his back. His dad was slowly improving and he was proud of him for fighting to regain his health. Just as he was about to

move away, Margret tried to hug him, but he jerked away
before she could touch him.

Margret looked stunned. Still, she composed herself.
"I haven't seen you in years," she said, staring up at him.

"Let's not pretend, Margret." Marcus looked her
over. "Why would I want to see you?"

Margret was about to say something, but Emily
announced dinner was ready. Marcus grabbed Karalee's
hand and quickly moved away.

At the large dining room table, everyone joined in
prayer. Afterwards, the room was full of laughter and
conversations about the past. It amazed Marcus how his
sister and brothers could talk to Margret like she'd never
done anything wrong. He could hardly eat his meal. He
started having flashbacks.

Unable to control himself, he threw his napkin on
the table.

"Are you okay?" his brother Jayden asked.

"No; I'm not." His voice rose. "Am I the only one at
this table who remembers how Margret used to treat us?
Or do all of my brothers and sister have amnesia?"

The room immediately became silent. He noticed his
six step brother's instantly looked defensive.

Jayden rested a hand on his thigh. "Bro; don't do
this. It's dad's birthday."

Marcus shook his head. "I need to get some fresh air," Marcus excused himself to the patio. He didn't even realize Karalee had followed him until she moved beside him and rubbed his back.

"Are you okay, babes?"

"I'll be fine. I just can't stand that woman."

"You can't keep running away from her," Karalee said, rubbing his arms. "Pull her aside and talk to her. Let her know how you feel."

He looked at Karalee. She was right. Since he'd been younger he'd been running and trying to avoid her. He wasn't a little boy anymore. He was a grown man who had a voice. For the first time in years, it was time to face his past.

Happy birthday echoed throughout the large family room. Marcus moved beside his dad. He and his brother's helped his dad blow out the candles, being he was too weak.

As Margret cut the cake, Marcus felt a rage he hadn't felt in a long time.

Seeing that fake smile on her face, as she passed out slices of cake, made him want to barf. How could she be so happy and radiant after all she'd done to him-his family? Why was he still so torn apart over it when she appeared to have moved on with her life?

The room broke out into applause, snapping him from his troubled thoughts.

Unable to contain his emotions, he moved into Emily's study. He stood in front of the fireplace and tried to think.

A knock sounded on the door. He was sure it was Karalee, but Margret walked in with two plates.

"What in the hell are you doing in here?" Marcus asked, ready to finish where he'd left off earlier.

"You didn't eat your dinner. I brought it along with a slice of cake." Margret sat both plates on the table.

"Are you crazy? I don't want anything from you." Marcus tried to move away, but she blocked him.

"Please, Marcus, can we talk?"

"About what?"

"Sit down and eat with me."

Marcus hesitated. The last thing he wanted to do was share a meal with an enemy, but finally, he decided it was time to get the load off of his chest. He sat and glared at her. "You know it's very funny that you brought me dinner. When I was younger, I always had to eat after you fed your children."

Margret squeezed her eyes closed. "I did some terrible things to you when you were younger." She paused and looked at him. "I'm sorry...so very sorry. I wanted to say that to you for a long time." She covered his hand with hers.

He snatched his hand away. "Why should I believe you are sorry?" Rage clouded his eyes. "Why shouldn't I believe you're not the same woman who shoved me onto the floor and caused me to injure my side?"

"Because I've been going to counseling since the day you left."

"What are you talking about?"

She dropped her sight to her plate and picked over the meal. "When you got hurt, I made your father send you away. I realized I needed help. I called your aunt too. I told her to take your brother's and sister. I didn't know what was wrong with me, and I was afraid of what I might do. When you all were gone, I immediately went into treatment. It took years, but I found out why I was so angry and hateful." She wiped tears from her eyes before continuing. "Marcus, I was physically and verbally abused when I was a child. When I became an adult, I had a lot of demons that I didn't know how to control. The abuse led me to do some very hurtful things to not only you and your family, but to everyone I came in contact with." Slowly she began to eat, talking in between. "Being in counseling helped me realize my wrongs. It helped me to not only heal from my past, but to go back and apologize to the people I'd wronged. I'm sorry for all the things I did. I'm asking you today to please forgive me."

Marcus shook his head as he watched her eat. "I don't know if I can do that, Margret."

"Maybe you could go to counseling with me."

He laughed. "I don't need help, lady. You do."

"You do too."

He pointed a finger at her. "Don't you dare turn what you did on me!"

"I'm not. I take full responsibility for what I did to you. All I'm suggesting is that we go to counseling as a family so we can all heal. I just want you to forgive me...please forgive me."

"This conversation is over," Marcus announced.

Margret dropped her face to her plate. She continued to eat as tears rolled off her face. Not feeling the least bit of sympathy, Marcus stood from the table and moved away.

He was about to exit when he heard banging.

Confused, he turned to Margret and noticed she was banging on the table.

"What is it now?" he asked, irritated. He moved back to her. It was then that he noticed her face was bright red and her eyes were budging out of her head. She continued to bang on the table. Then she wrapped her hand around her throat.

She was choking! Without thinking, he moved behind her.

The door to the study opened and Emily walked in.

"She's chocking! Call 911!" Marcus shouted.

Emily rushed out of the room while Marcus lifted her and began the Heimlich maneuver. But no matter how much he thrust-nothing. Soon the study was packed with worried, frantic family members. On the eight thrust, the steak flew from her mouth, but Margret was limp, not breathing and unconscious. By then Ford, who was also a Cardiologist, had stepped in to begin CPR.

Questions abounded.

Marcus tried to answer the questions, but he was confused and scared. He'd never been more frightened in his life. Karalee tried to comfort him as he waited. He could barely breathe. He hoped and prayed Margret would survive.

"She's breathing!" Ford finally shouted after what seemed like an eternity.

Weakly, Marcus sat. Sweat covered his body and his hands wouldn't stop shaking. The EMS rushed into the room and took over.

Soon, they were rolling Margret out on a stretcher.

Marcus was met with hugs and handshakes as he exited the study behind EMS.

"Thank God you were in there to help her," Emily said, resting her hand on his shoulder. "I'm proud of you."

Marcus was still in shock as the family scurried out of the door to head for the hospital. He had always said he wouldn't spit on Margret if she was on fire, but when he'd realized she was choking, all of his hate went out of the window. If she would have died, he would have never gotten over the fact that her last words were for him to forgive her. Those words would have plagued his mind forever.

Just as he was about to head out the door, a wheelchair blocked him from moving. It was Carlos. The two men stared at each other for a few seconds. Marcus didn't expect the extended hand Carlos held out to him or the hug when he pulled him down to him.

"I was on the balcony," Carlos revealed. "I heard everything." He shook his head. "I had no idea that happened to you when you were younger, man. I'm sorry and I love you, cuz."

Marcus felt tears in his eyes as he wrapped his arms tighter around Carlos. "I love you too," he said, feeling himself getting choked up.

When he pulled away, he noticed Carlos had tears on his face. "Hey; do you think you can help me apply for college next week?"

Marcus eyes widened in surprise. He squeezed his hand. "Of course I will."

Marcus moved outside, hand in hand with Karalee just as the EMS was about to close the door. He stopped them and asked could he speak with Margret.

He climb inside the ambulance and kneeled beside her. Her eyes were halfway open and there was a mask over her face. He knelt beside her and grabbed her hand. She focused her weak eyes on him.

"I just want you to know that I forgive you, Margret," he said with sincerity. He lowered his face. "Maybe after you start feeling better, we can talk about going to counseling."

He noticed tears in her eyes and she squeezed his hand.

When he left the ambulance, the biggest load was lifted off of his chest. Emily was right. No amount of boxing could help him feel the peace he felt now. Only forgiveness had.

That night, Karalee lay on Marcus's chest in his bed. They had just made love, and she could feel his heart still racing as they collected their breaths. As her body returned to normal, she thought of all that had happened that day.

"I'm so proud of you, Marcus," she said, kissing his chest."

"Why?"

"It takes a big man to forgive the person who hurt you."

"I'm just thankful Margret survived so I could let her know I'd forgiven her." He lifted her chin. "Are you okay?"

"I'm fine. What happened today just made me think."

"About what?"

"I've been angry with Chris for so long. I'm only hurting myself by holding on to the past. He's moved on with his life and I'm the one stuck."

"It's strange that I learned that same lesson today." Marcus squeezed his eyes shut.

"I'm not gonna be mad anymore," Karalee decided. "Neither will I hold what happened to me in the past against you."

"What do you mean?"

"I've been afraid to let you help me, Marcus. And it was all because of what Chris did to me." She squeezed his hand. "You're not my ex. I'm not going to punish you for what he did anymore. I'm tired of holding on to that fear and being afraid because of what he did to me."

"Then let it go. Let it go right now, Karalee."

She looked up at him and smiled. "I just did," she said, letting out a deep sigh.

19

A few days later, Marcus drove Karalee to Summer's house to help her pack up the things she'd brought for her mother. When they pulled close to the house, they saw flashing police cars.

Karalee jumped from the SUV and ran toward the house. Millions of thoughts ran through her mind. Had something happened to Summer? Maybe she'd had another flare up with Lupus.

When she entered the house, everything was in disarray. Police were inside. Summer was sitting on the chair with Spider whose arms were wrapped around her as she sobbed.

"Summer what happened?" Karalee stumbled to her.

Summer shook her head. "Mom…"

"What about mom?" Karalee's voice trembled.

"Mom's dead. They found her in an alley. She overdosed."

"No!" Karalee mumbled, backing up. When her legs collapsed, Marcus was there to catch her.

Marcus held Karalee in his arms for the rest of the night as she cried. "It's my fault."

"Baby, it's not your fault."

"I sent her money to catch a train and she used it to get high…she overdosed."

Marcus massaged her forehead as she rested on his lap. "You had good intentions, Karalee. You were trying to help her. You had no idea she would use that money you sent her in that way, anymore than I had any idea Carlos would get on my bike and hurt himself. You should not feel guilty. You gave your all to try to help her, and you should have peace because of that."

"I don't know how I'm going to get over this." Karalee continued to cry.

"You will; I'm not letting you leave my side until you do."

Karalee never imagined the next time she saw her mother she'd be in a casket. The pain was so intense; she didn't know how she made it through the next few days. She felt so much regret and hurt. She would never see her mother again, or hear her voice. She wished she'd never sent the money, and she wished she would have talked with her longer on the telephone that day she'd call.

The only thing she could do was make sure she was put away nicely. Marcus went all out to ensure that was done. Her mother was put together so nicely in the casket that it looked like she'd gotten dressed in her

Sunday best, and drifted off to sleep. She looked completely at peace. Karalee made sure she was buried next to her grandma.

For the next few days, she grieved. Thankfully she had Marcus and Summer to support her. If it wasn't for them she seriously doubted she would have made it.

A week after the funeral, Karalee was still in the dumps. She stayed to herself, grieving and trying to come to terms with the tragedy. Marcus knew how to lift her sprits. He took her to Lee's lake. It would be a weekend of relaxation and rejuvenation.

After they set up camp, he grabbed her hand and took her for a walk.

"I remember the first time we came here," he reminisced.

Karalee smiled. "So do I. You didn't know what to expect."

"Yeah, but now I love this place." Marcus wrapped his arm around her waist. "I love you too. He and Karalee stopped and shared a delicious kiss.

"I want you to see something," he said, grabbing her hand again. He led her to the sitting area and the tall tree beside it.

"Notice anything different about the tree?" He asked, standing behind her as she moved to it.

Karalee studied it. "My grandmother and granddad's name are still there." She gasped. "Marcus, our name is engraved on this tree."

He watched as she outline the heart shaped etched with their names in the center.

"When did you do this?"

He pulled the tiny box from his pocket and dropped to his knee just as she turned to him.

She gasped and tears filled her eyes.

"Karalee, I want our children to come here sixty years from now and see our names on this tree. I love you with all my heart; I can't live without you. Please say you will marry me?"

"Yes, I'll marry you," she said, unable to hold in her tears as she jumped in his arms. He felt his pounding heart rate increase even more as they kissed. When they were done, he slid the massive ring onto her finger.

A few days later, Karalee went to Summer's house to get the rest of her things. The house was empty. Summer had told her that she and Spider would be at the hospital for that entire day having test done. She packed the boxes in the basement room, filling them with the things she'd gotten for her mother. Things her mother would never see or wear. She didn't realize she was crying until she felt the tears on her cheeks. She plopped down on the bed and grabbed tissue to wipe her cheeks. Afterwards, she took a sip from her glass of punch. Unexpectedly, Snow White jumped on the bed, causing her to waste the juice on her light colored pants.

"Bad girl," she said, standings and chastising the cat. She placed the glass on the table and grabbed a change of clothes before heading to the basement bathroom. She stripped and turned on the water. No water would come out.

"Great," she muttered, hating the wet, sticky feel of the liquid on her skin.

She slipped on her robe and moved upstairs to her sister's room.

Entering the bedroom, she closed the door and moved into the bathroom. She turned on the shower. The water came out, and she adjusted the knobs to make it warm.

Slipping off her robe, she stepped inside. Just a few minutes and she would be cleaned. She lathered her body down with soap and then rinsed it away. When she was done, she turned off the shower. Suddenly, the shower door opened, startling her. Her eyes enlarged in horror when she realized it was Spider. He was standing outside completely naked.

"What the hell are you doing?"

He laughed and began stroking his shaft. "What you and I both wanted to do all along."

Karalee could hear her heart beating in her chest. He'd been home all the time, watching her! "Get out!" She used her hands to try to cover her naked body. When he wouldn't move, she attempted to shove past him. But he stepped in and grabbed her by the throat, pinning her against the wall.

Ignoring her screams, he used his knee and forced her legs apart, kissing her neck as he held her against the wall.

"What in the hell is going on!"

Spider jerked away and Karalee saw Summer standing in the bathroom doorway. Crying hysterically, Karalee slid down the bathroom wall.

Spider rushed out of the shower. "Baby, I was in here taking a shower and she got in here with me," he lied. He covered his lower body with a towel.

"He's lying, Summer!" Karalee sobbed. "I was taking a shower and he came in here with me!"

"Get out!" Summer shouted while Karalee covered her trembling flesh with the robe. She shouted it three times before Karalee realized she was saying it to her.

"You believe him?" Karalee asked incredulously.

"Just leave!" Summer shouted.

"You think I'd do something like that? You're my only sister. I would never do anything to hurt you!"

"You got five minutes to get out of my house." Summer warned.

Karalee burst into tears all over again. "Summer…please."

Summer turned her face away. Karalee staggered out of the bathroom. She didn't even bother to change out of the robe. She found her car keys and rushed outside into the SUV, exceeding the speed limit as she drove away.

Marcus didn't know what was going on when Karalee burst into his front door sobbing.

"Karalee!" He rushed behind her as she hurried into his bathroom and jumped into the shower. She adjusted the water to hot and got inside and began scrubbing her body.

Karalee… baby; what's wrong?" Marcus's heart was beating out of his chest. He turned off the water and got into the shower, catching her when she collapsed to the floor in tears.

He took her face into his hands and looked into her eyes. "Baby, what happened? What's wrong? Talk to me!" He shook her lightly.

"Spider…"

Marcus felt his heart increase to a pass out level. "Spider what?" he asked. "Talk to me!"

Karalee sobbed out the entire story.

"I'm going to kill him!" Seeing double, Marcus thundered out of the shower and headed for the door. Just as he opened it, Karalee stopped him.

"No! Marcus...please don't do anything to get in trouble!"

"Move, Karalee!" he shouted, feeling out of his mind. He gently pushed her aside.

Karalee wrapped her arms around his waist. "No, I need you! Please don't leave me!"

The words snapped him to his senses.

He took her into his arms. "I'm sorry, baby." He kissed her forehead and held her as she sobbed in his arms.

It took Marcus hours to calm Karalee down enough for her to fall sleep.

When he heard her light snores, he eased from the bed. Hopefully, he would be back before she awoke. He had business to take care of.

Spider heard the doorbell ring. He moved from the living room couch. He had barely escaped being kicked out on the streets a few hours earlier. Summer had been gone for hours. She'd left an hour after Karalee, but not without questioning him like a detective. Thankfully, she had believed him over Karalee.

From the day he'd seen Karalee, he'd wanted her. He cared about Summer, but really she was just a place to lay low and someone who would pay bills for him and take care of his child support.

The doorbell rung again.

"Hold up; I'm coming," he shouted. He opened the door.

He recognized the muscular man outside on the porch. It was Marcus Tucker. He knew what he wanted; still he told him Summer was not there.

"I'm not here to see Summer."

"Then what you want, man?"

"That incident you pulled today."

Without warning, Spider felt the wind get knocked out of him. He grabbed his throat. Marcus had chopped him in the neck. For a few seconds everything went dark and he was on the floor, paralyzed and unable to breath.

Marcus towered over him for a few seconds, before kneeling over him. "Don't you ever come near here again!"

The last thing Spider remembered before everything went dark was the powerful punch that burned his face.

***

Summer found her front door wide open. She hurried inside. Spider was knocked out cold on the floor with a swollen black eye.

She shook him and slowly he roused, whimpering in pain.

"What happened?" Summer questioned.

"Marcus came over here… he hit me in the throat and knocked me out."

Summer moved past him, not helping him from the floor.

"Baby, I'm pressing charges against him." Spider limped to the sofa and sat. "Grab me some ice."

Summer's blood pressure was off the charts as she moved to the kitchen. "You want some ice?" She grabbed the ice bucket and moved back into the living room. "Yeah; you need some ice to cool off; you son of a bitch!" She tossed the ice on him, causing him to jump up.

"What the hell is wrong with you?" Spider shouted.

"I want you to leave!"

"Baby…what's wrong? What's gotten into you?"

Summer tossed the ice bucket at him, barely missing his head. "You're a liar…a bum!" She rushed to the bedroom and came back with his clothes, tossing them at him.

Spider picked his clothes up off the floor.

"It's like that. You putting me out."

"Yeah; I took your name off of everything too. I don't want to see your sorry ass again!"

"Alright, I'm out." Spider grabbed his clothes and rushed out the door.

When the door closed, Summer dropped on the chair. Sobs shook her body.

***

Karalee awoke to find Marcus right by her side. She smiled weakly and grabbed his hand. "I'm sorry, Marcus."

"For what?"

"You were right. I should have listened to you. I shouldn't have been so damn set in my ways of being independent. If I would have left Summer's house when you asked me, this wouldn't have happened."

He shushed her with a kiss.

"Baby, no one will ever hurt you again. That's my promise," he said, before sealing it with a kiss.

20

A month later, Karalee tried to breathe normally. Her heart had been fluttering all day. She felt so beautiful in her white silk wedding gown. She heard the wedding music playing.

"Are you ready?" Emily asked.

"Yes," she said, taking in a deep breath. She looped her arm into Emily's husband Stanley's. Being she didn't have a father, he had agreed to give her away. Karalee felt sad that she had no family at her wedding. Summer had not accepted her invitation. Still she shook it from her memory and started down the aisle.

The church was packed, but all she could see was Marcus. His eyes were wet and his smile a mile long.

As the preacher said the sermon, tears slid down Marcus's face causing Karalee to cry. Before the pastor could say 'you may now kiss the bride' they were in each other arms. The crowd erupted into cheers.

Afterwards, the two headed outside to the limo that would take them to the reception hall. Karalee noticed a familiar face outside, standing on the side walk. It was Summer!

"I invited her," Marcus, squeezed her hand. Tears covered Karalee's eyes as she moved to her sister and gave her a tight hug.

Summer pulled away and grabbed her hands." You sure are a pretty bride."

Karalee laughed as more tears fell.

"I want you to know I'm sorry. I knew you were telling the truth when you told me. I was just so-"

Karalee shushed her. "I forgive you. Please come to the reception."

"I'll be there." Summer gave her another tight hug.

Karalee moved back to Marcus. He took her hand and guided her to the limo.

"Once inside, he pulled her face to his." He pressed her body to his, feeling his nature twitch.

"Whoa boy," Karalee whispered into his ear. "We have the entire honeymoon for that."

"I can't wait," he said, forcing himself to regain control.

At the reception, Marcus was surrounded by his brothers and sister. His father and stepmom were there too along with Carlos.

Karalee had just thrown the bouquet. The women fought like animals over it. Finally a woman named Fatima won.

Marcus shook his head, hoping the men would be more civil. Karalee sat on the chair. The single men gathered around them on the dance floor. The man who caught the garter would get to dance with Fatima being she'd caught the bouquet.

"Aright gentleman; let's see who's next to get married," Marcus teased.

He lifted Karalee's dress and slid off the garter.

The men laughed and cheered as he tossed it over his shoulder. When he turned, he noticed his brother Jayden had caught it.

He walked to him and hugged his shoulder. "Well guys, we know who is getting married next." The entire room erupted in laughter as Jayden and Fatima moved onto the dance floor together.

Marcus moved to his new wife. He guided her onto the dance floor, ready to dance the night away.

"Are you ready to spend your life with me?" Karalee asked.

Marcus kissed her and looked deeply into her eyes. "Of course," he said seriously. "You were made for me, and I was made to love you."

Dear Readers,

Thank you for reading, Sent From Heaven 2. Please visit my website:

www.deedeemscott.com

www.ahsyadpublication.com

Facebook: Ahsyad Publication Bookreaders

God bless and thanks again for the support!

www.ingramcontent.com/pod-product-compliance
Lightning Source LLC
Chambersburg PA
CBHW030030180626
46810CB00001B/301